"I don't know if I
this way."

"I'll make sure your fac[...]
Your eyes, anyway. N[...]

"Except you and me."

She wished she could see what he was seeing now.
She wasn't some model—just an ordinary woman
with a far from perfect figure. She was crazy to do
this. "Jake, I—" She started to sit up.

"No. Lie still. You're beautiful." The shutter clicked,
the auto-winder whirred. Once, twice, half a
dozen times.

"Jake, please. This feels so strange."

"Why? I've seen you naked before."

"But you've never...stared at me like this. From
across the room." She shifted her hips, trying to
get more comfortable, but the discomfort she felt
was inside her, not in her surroundings. "I feel like
I'm on display."

"And I like what I see."

Dear Reader,

Ah, summer vacation! The perfect chance to relax, have fun and try something new. When Glynna McCormick takes advantage of a weekend on a fantasy island to seduce wild man Jake Dawson, she discovers a whole new side of herself— and the man of her dreams.

While most of us don't have quite that much excitement on our vacations, it is always nice to get away for a while. This book was inspired by my own once-in-a-lifetime trip to a romantic, couples-only resort in Jamaica. Not only did my husband and I have a fantastic time, but also we made friends with some other wonderful couples we still keep in touch with today.

Whether your vacation is a trip to Disneyland, a day at the beach or a relaxing afternoon in your own backyard, I hope you'll find some time to rest and relax during the year…maybe with a good book, like this one!

I love to hear from readers. E-mail me at cindi@cindimyers.com or visit my Web site, www.CindiMyers.com.

Cindi Myers

Books by Cindi Myers

HARLEQUIN BLAZE
82—JUST 4 PLAY
118—RUMOR HAS IT

HARLEQUIN FLIPSIDE
10—LIFE ACCORDING TO LUCY
20—WHAT PHOEBE WANTS

HARLEQUIN TEMPTATION
902—IT'S A GUY THING!
935—SAY YOU WANT ME

TAKING IT ALL OFF

Cindi Myers

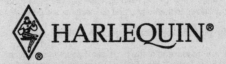

HARLEQUIN®

TORONTO • NEW YORK • LONDON
AMSTERDAM • PARIS • SYDNEY • HAMBURG
STOCKHOLM • ATHENS • TOKYO • MILAN • MADRID
PRAGUE • WARSAW • BUDAPEST • AUCKLAND

For the Tower Island Gang

ISBN 0-373-79153-4

TAKING IT ALL OFF

www.eHarlequin.com

Printed in U.S.A.

1

FROM NOW ON, we're going to do things differently.

Sure we are, Glynna thought as she read through the memo from Gordon McCormick—aka her father—about his plans to revamp *Texas Style,* the biweekly magazine he'd overseen for the past twenty-five years. Glynna had no doubt the magazine would change—her dad had already hired a new managing editor and a new art director, determined to transform the ailing publication's stodgy reputation and lagging sales. What wasn't likely to be any different was her own role as staff drudge.

She looked at her cluttered desktop. How had she gotten so far away from her real love, writing? Sure, she still produced articles for the magazine, but those were squeezed in between the rest of the tasks her dad assigned her. And what about the other work she wanted to do—the hard-hitting investigative stories that could really launch her career to the top? She had half a dozen such pieces crammed into file folders on her desk, clamoring for time she didn't have to give them.

She frowned at the thick folder on top of her in-box—reader surveys her father wanted her to summarize in a report. A report he would glance at once, then ignore. Contemplating that folder made her queasy.

Sucking in a deep breath, she picked up the file and dropped it in her trash can. She smiled at the sight of it balanced atop the fast-food wrappers and disposable coffee cups, relief stealing over her.

But the pleasure was short-lived, as her well-honed sense of obligation took over. What would her father say if he saw it?

Overwhelmed by guilt, she fished out the folder and put it back in her in-box. Having a conscience was a pain in the ass sometimes.

Her intercom buzzer sounded. "Glynna, can I see you in my office when you have a free minute?" Editor Stacy Southern's pleasant voice brought a smile to Glynna's lips. Here was one thing her dad had done that actually made Glynna's life easier. Stacy was a great editor and a true gal pal. The two women had bonded the day Stacy had interviewed for the editor's position. Glynna had found her in the ladies' room, frantically trying to stop a run in her stockings.

One new pair of panty hose and two aspirin later, Stacy had the job and Glynna had a new best friend.

She leaned forward and punched the button for Stacy's office. "I'll be right over." Any excuse to get away from that overflowing in-box for a while.

She headed toward Stacy's office, turning the corner just as the stairway door burst open and a familiar figure in motorcycle leathers barely missed colliding with her. He jerked back just in time, though the saddlebag slung over his shoulder popped open, spilling manila envelopes across the floor at her feet.

"Hey, sorry." Jake Dawson, staff photographer and

unconventional thorn in her father's side, reached out to steady her. "I didn't expect anybody to be out here."

She shrugged out of his grasp, the leather of his fingerless gloves dragging against the silk of her blouse. With the ends of his shoulder-length blond hair tangled by the wind and his jacket unzipped to reveal a Museum of Modern Art T-shirt, Jake stood out amidst the suited office workers like a cobra in a cage of pigeons. And he was about as dangerous, at least to her sense of well-being. He had the annoying ability to fluster her, in spite of her best efforts to remain cool. Maybe it was the unnerving way his steel-blue gaze met hers directly, as if daring her to hide anything from him. Or the obvious enjoyment he got from refusing to adhere to any accepted standard of corporate behavior.

Or maybe it was the heat that built within her whenever he was near, an unbidden flicker of desire that reminded her that she was a woman and Jake was a man with a capital *M*. A man she didn't want anything to do with, despite the automatic way her body responded to him. Why was it she could control everything else about her life but the way this one man made her feel?

"Where are you off to in such a hurry?" She hid her agitation by stooping and picking up a handful of the envelopes that had slipped from his bag. As she rose, one of them opened and a black and white photograph slid to the floor.

She stared at the photo, warmth flooding her face as she realized it was the image of a nude woman—a full-breasted, round-hipped woman seated in a chair, hair falling across her face, hiding her identity, while her spread-legged posture left nothing else to the imagination.

"Do you mind?" Jake eased the photo from her hand.

"Wh—what are you doing with those?" Glynna stepped back, struggling to remain calm, though her heart beat wildly and tension coiled between her thighs.

Jake glanced at the photo, a half smile on his lips. "Didn't anyone tell you? We figured it would really increase the readership of *Texas Style* if we started including centerfolds."

Typical Jake. He could never give a straight answer. Fine. She could play his game. "Uh-huh. And of course, you volunteered to do all the photography."

"Of course."

"And is that some of your work?" She nodded to the photograph, struggling not to stare at the arresting image. It was erotic, without being pornographic. Artistic, even. Not that she was an expert or anything....

"As a matter of fact, it is." He slipped the photo back into the envelope and replaced it in his bag. When he looked at her again, his expression was teasing. "Maybe you'd care to pose for me sometime? Bet your dad would like that, huh?"

She stiffened, even as her nipples tightened at the thought of getting naked with Jake. "What does my father have to do with it? Not that I have any intention of 'posing' for you."

He shrugged. "No surprise there. You're daddy's girl, after all." His gaze traveled up her legs, across her torso, lingering on her breasts before meeting her eyes once more. "It's a shame, really."

He turned and sauntered down the hall, his boot heels making muffled thuds on the carpet.

Glynna stared after him. "What do you mean by that?" But she spoke too softly for him to hear her.

Not that she didn't already have an idea of what his answer would be. Jake had made no secret of the fact that he thought she and her father were uptight, image-obsessed corporate clones "who wouldn't know fun and sexy if it climbed up on the conference table and did a dance." Or such had been his assessment at the last staff meeting he'd been forced to attend.

If he wasn't such a brilliant photographer, her father would have fired him weeks ago. But brilliance—and advertiser and reader praise—could convince a publisher to overlook a lot.

On shaky legs, she continued down the corridor toward Stacy's office. Jake was a gifted photographer. His work had won recognition from the Texas Press Association and he'd garnered awards in regional shows. So why was he taking pictures of naked women? Was the woman in the photo a model—or a girlfriend?

She frowned, ignoring the sudden sinking feeling in her stomach. What difference did it make to her? No doubt Jake Dawson had a string of model-girlfriends eager to pose for him. Women who were as "fun and sexy" as Glynna wasn't.

Pondering this disturbing thought, she knocked on Stacy's open door.

"Glynna! Come in." Smiling, Stacy turned from her computer to greet her friend. A thirty-something blonde with a reputation for making change happen, Stacy had been hired to turn things around at the ailing magazine. But already she and Gordon had butted heads over what direction *Texas Style* should take. Glynna figured the battle would be interesting, as long as she herself stayed out of the line of fire.

She settled in the chair in front of Stacy's desk and slipped out of her high heels. "What's up?"

"The usual Monday morning chaos." Stacy nodded at the pile of paper in front of her. "Did you have a good weekend?"

Glynna shrugged. Her typical weekend was spent working on copy for the magazine, cleaning her condo and having Sunday dinner with her father. Nothing exciting there. "The usual." Let Stacy make of that what she would.

Stacy arched one perfect brow. "No hot dates? Sexy men? Wild adventures?"

Glynna laughed out loud. "Since when does any of that apply to me?" When she did date, she favored conservative, bookish types. Not particularly thrilling, but the playing field wasn't that broad in her social circle.

Stacy made a noncommittal noise and opened a file folder in front of her. "Was that Jake Dawson I heard in the hall just now?"

Glynna silently cursed the hot flush that rose to her face. "Yes."

"Mmmm. Now there's a sexy man for you. Gorgeous, smart, talented and a little crazy." Stacy grinned. "You wouldn't have a boring weekend with him."

"I wouldn't have *any* kind of weekend with him." Glynna sat up straighter, ignoring the flutter in her stomach at the thought of a date with wild man Jake Dawson. "Honestly. He's not my type and I'm sure he wouldn't be interested in someone like me."

"What do you mean, someone like you? Attractive, smart and talented. Sounds to me like the two of you have a lot in common."

Glynna crossed, then uncrossed her legs. "You've been working too hard, Stace. You're imagining things." She leaned forward, eager to change the subject. "So what did you want to see me about?"

"Oh, you're gonna love this." Stacy riffled through the folder and pulled out a slick color brochure. "Take a look."

Glynna glanced at the picture of a photogenic young couple clad in teeny, tiny swimsuits, lounging in the surf. *What's your romantic fantasy?* the brochure asked.

She turned the page. An elaborate sandcastle-like structure sat on a beach where palm trees swayed and more young couples frolicked in the surf. "At La Paloma Resort, fantasies do come true," she read from the brochure. "La Paloma? I've never heard of the place." She slid the brochure back to Stacy. "Is it one of those Caribbean places for honeymooners?"

"You're almost right. It's a new couples-only resort on Paloma Island—off the coast of Galveston. The grand opening is this weekend, and we've been invited to send a reporter to cover it."

"Why? I mean, I guess a new resort is nice, but it's not exactly the kind of thing *Texas Style* usually covers."

"Exactly. The old *Texas Style* would have had a one-paragraph blurb buried in the back of the magazine, behind an article on some oil baron's redecorating project and a piece on downtown steak restaurants. Which explains why sales figures are plunging to the basement." She picked up a hefty stack of computer printouts and shook them at Glynna. "If we want to attract more advertisers, we need to attract younger, hipper, sexier readers. And that means hipper, sexier articles."

"But a new resort?"

"Not just a new resort. I'm thinking of a cover article with the theme 'romantic fantasies.' Something sexy and fun."

Glynna shook her head. The typical *Texas Style* cover story focused on the upcoming opera season or the dismal state of oil futures or other topics deemed of interest to Houston's Old Guard upper class. "My dad will never go for it."

"Which is why I don't intend to tell him until it's too late to do anything about it." Stacy leaned toward Glynna. "There's not going to *be* a *Texas Style* magazine if we don't do something drastic, and soon. The competition is killing us. But an article like this, done right, will get people talking about us. That kind of buzz translates into readers and ad dollars. Your father may balk at first, but he'll thank me later."

Glynna sighed. "You're right. Dad is set in his ways, but he's a good businessman. He won't argue with results."

"Great." Stacy sat back, smiling. "Be at Pier Six at nine o'clock Friday morning. The resort's yacht will transport you to La Paloma."

"Yacht?" Glynna stood. "What are you talking about?"

"The grand opening? I told you they've invited a reporter to attend, to write about the resort."

Glynna jumped to her feet. "But it doesn't have to be me! Didn't you say this was couples only? And I'm an investigative reporter. Romance isn't my thing."

"Then maybe it's time you 'investigated' the topic." Stacy set aside the computer printouts and leaned toward Glynna. "I'm taking a real risk here. This story has to be stellar if I'm going to pull this off. I need my best writer—and that's you."

"I'm flattered, but really…"

"No buts. I've already given them your name. Besides, I think you could use a little time off." Stacy sat back and gave her a long look. "When was the last time you had a vacation?"

Glynna couldn't meet her gaze. Her father rarely took time off, and she'd felt obligated to follow his example. She told herself she'd have time for vacations later, when she was further along in her career. Right now, she had too much work to do.

"This wouldn't exactly be a vacation," she said. "Not if I'm supposed to be reporting."

"There's no reason you can't have fun, too." Stacy shoved the brochure back across the desk. "This place has a private beach, gourmet restaurants, nightly entertainment, even a spa." She smiled. "You can take a few days R & R and write a killer story. Besides, I know you don't have anything else planned for this weekend."

Glynna sighed. Stacy knew her too well. "All right. I'll go. But you owe me."

Stacy grinned. "You never know. After this weekend,

you may feel like you owe me. After all, anything could happen in a romantic paradise."

"I'm going to *work,* Stace. I'll come home with a story, nothing else."

Stacy laughed. "Then maybe you should try harder."

JAKE'S BOOTS pounded against the carpet as he made his way toward art director Nick Castillo's office. He'd been annoyed by Nick's abrupt summons, and more annoyed still by his encounter just now with Glynna McCormick. Something about the woman always set him on edge.

For one thing, she was as uptight as her old man. He hadn't missed the way her lips tightened in disapproval when she'd seen the photo. She was what—twenty-five? Twenty-six? Hadn't she seen another woman naked before?

Had she seen a *man* naked? He couldn't recall any office gossip about her dating, but he'd only been with the magazine a short time. He didn't need any longer than that to have Glynna figured out. Her "don't touch me" attitude probably kept most men far away. He knew the type—blue-blood princesses who thought they were better than everyone else. She needed a real man to rock her world. To show her what that sexy bod of hers was made for.

He shook off the thought as he turned down the hallway leading to Nick's office. Why was he thinking about Glynna? He could care less if her world was rocked or not. He had more important things to think about, like getting ready for his first major gallery show.

Nick was barking orders into the phone when Jake poked his head around the door. The art director motioned him closer. "I know how much it costs and I don't care!" Nick growled. "I'll worry about the budget, you worry about doing what I want."

Jake dropped his saddlebag on the floor, settled into the plush leather chair across from Nick's desk and stretched his long legs out in front of him. As soon as the art director hung up the phone, he said, "What's the big rush to get me down here this morning? I've got half a dozen more important things to do."

"Yeah. Yeah. You're the big-shot *artiste*. Don't give me that bullshit." Nick tented his fingers and grinned at Jake. "You won't be so annoyed when you hear what I've cooked up for you."

"Let me guess. You want me to shoot the Grand Champion Steer at the Stock Show? Isn't that always a big deal here at *Texas Style?*"

Nick laughed. "Maybe in the past, but no more." He leaned forward. "What would you think of an eight-page photo essay? Something edgy and artsy—right up your alley."

Jake tempered the jitter of excitement that shot through him. "That's pretty radical for this place. Did Stacy agree?"

"She doesn't know yet. But I'll talk her into it."

Jake shook his head. "I don't know, Nick. Stacy isn't one of your little girlfriends you can sweet-talk into anything."

"No, but she's smart." Nick sat back, smiling slightly. "And beneath her hard-nosed facade, she's still a woman." His smile widened. "A damned attractive one, even if she isn't my type. I'll make her see that this is the kind of thing we need to move ahead of the competition."

"What about McCormick?"

Nick frowned. "What about him? He said he wanted to revamp the publication. This is what it takes."

Jake picked up his saddlebag and slung it over his shoulder. "I can't believe you called me into your office for this crap. Next time, leave a message on my desk."

"Wait. I do have something for you." He tossed a brochure at him.

Jake caught the glossy flyer and stared at the young couple making out on the front. "La Paloma Resort? What do you want me to do with this?"

"It's the cover story for the next issue. A luxury, couples-only resort on Paloma Island. I want you to go there this weekend and shoot the photos."

Jake scanned the brochure copy, which promised sun, sand and sex. Except that if the place catered to couples, he wasn't likely to find much of the third. Still, a few days lounging on the beach, aiming his camera at bikini-clad babes didn't sound bad. "Who's writing the story?"

"Who else? Ace reporter Glynna McCormick."

He frowned. Just what he needed—a weekend surrounded by cooing honeymooners while he was saddled with the ice princess.

"What's the matter? Don't think you can handle a few days with the boss's daughter?"

He tossed the brochure back on Nick's desk. "You take care of Stacy. I'll deal with Glynna." He'd make sure she knew he expected her to stay out of his way. Once they laid out the ground rules, there'd be no trouble at all.

2

GLYNNA SET HER ALARM to go off an hour early Friday morning. While she filled a suitcase with swimsuits, sundresses and sandals, she returned three phone calls from business associates, and made dinner reservations for her father and a client at his favorite restaurant. Then she faxed the reservation information and some marketing projections he'd asked her to compile to his office, so they'd be waiting for him when he came in promptly at eight o'clock.

She was headed to her car when she remembered she was supposed to call the dry cleaners to ask them to deliver her father's suits to his office. She started to turn around and head back upstairs to retrieve the number, then stopped herself. Her father was a grown man. It wouldn't kill him to call about his own cleaning.

Buoyed by this minor rebellion, she drove ten miles over the speed limit and joined the crowd gathered at Pier Six in Galveston with two minutes to spare.

She stepped into the sea of hand-holding couples dressed in tropical prints and khaki and felt like the lone unicorn in line for the ark. "There you are," said a familiar, masculine voice. "I was beginning to think you weren't going to make it."

She whirled and almost collided with Jake Dawson. Dressed in khaki shorts, a Shiner Bock beer T-shirt and sandals, his shaggy hair tousled by the ocean breeze, he might have been a frat boy on vacation. Only the scuffed leather camera bag slung over his shoulder hinted that he wasn't your typical beachcomber. "What are you doing here?" she asked.

He hefted the bag. "I couldn't pass up the opportunity to shoot you in a swimsuit." His gaze took in the tailored sundress that left her shoulders and legs bare. "This is the first time I've seen you out of the corporate uniform." He grinned. "I like it."

"As if I was really worried about your opinion," she said, even as her cheeks warmed in a blush she told herself had nothing to do with his praise or the way his eyes continued to linger on her. She turned away from him, facing out over the bay. A stiff breeze tugged at her hair, bringing the scents of salt, fish and diesel fumes from the shrimp boats trawling in the distance. "Stacy didn't tell me she'd assigned you to photograph this story."

"She said she wanted the best. That would be me."

His arrogance grated, but Glynna had to admit the truth in his words. She should have known Stacy would want their top photographer for this piece. Fine. They each had separate jobs to do. It wasn't as if they'd be spending a lot of time together this weekend.

"Here's the *Queen Mary* now." Jake moved to stand beside her and nodded toward the large white yacht steaming toward them. He let out a low whistle. "Must be some money in this romantic fantasy business."

"Do you have something against romance?" she asked.

He adjusted the bag on his shoulder. "Let's just say my idea of what's romantic doesn't necessarily coincide with the hearts-and-flowers schmaltz that's marketed as such." He cut his eyes to her. "What about you? Underneath that stern exterior, do you harbor secret longings for pink cupids, red roses and tear-jerking love ballads?"

A laugh escaped her before she quite knew what was happening. His pleased grin sent a rush of warmth through her. She shook her head, still chuckling. "Cupids and ballads I can do without. But what woman doesn't like roses?"

The yacht had docked and was tying off, so she picked up her suitcase and followed the other couples toward it. Jake strode after her. "Roses are so predictable," he said. "I thought you'd have more imagination."

She started to tell him she'd be happy with any flowers any man took the trouble to send her, but thought better of it. She'd had little experience with romance in her life, but he didn't need to know that.

A Captain Davies welcomed them aboard the *Freebird.* "Our travel time to La Paloma is about twenty minutes, so sit back and make yourselves comfortable," he said.

Glynna settled onto a cushioned bench in the bow and Jake sat beside her, his hip almost touching hers. She wanted to move over, but they were sandwiched between pairs of cuddling newlyweds, so she settled for avoiding looking at him, focusing instead on the white-capped waves scudding toward them. The wind had picked up, and she was forced to twist her hair to one side and hold it back to keep it from whipping into her eyes.

The motor started and the yacht eased out of the slip, then turned and headed across the bay. Glynna gasped as the boat rose and fell in the rough seas. Waves slapped against the hull and spray arched back over the bow, splashing her feet.

Her stomach rolled with the boat, and she wondered if skipping breakfast had been such a good idea. Then again, if she'd eaten, would she feel even worse?

She clenched her teeth and closed her eyes, determined not to embarrass herself by being seasick in front of Jake and all these strangers.

"Don't close your eyes." His voice was soft in her ear as he took her hand in his.

Her eyes snapped open and she turned to stare at him. "What are you doing?"

"Don't close your eyes. It'll only make things worse."

She pulled her hand from his and smoothed it down her knee. "I'm fine."

"You don't look it. You're a sickly gray color and you're sweating." He put his hands on her shoulders and faced her forward. "Focus on the horizon, not the waves. That will help."

She did as he suggested, though her stomach still threatened to betray her.

"You never answered me about the roses," he said, his hands still on her shoulders, his face so close to hers she could feel his breath on the back of her neck. "Are they really your favorite?"

She blinked at this sudden change of subject and tried to think. "Dahlias," she said after a moment. "I like dahlias."

"Why do you like them?"

"I don't know." She shook her head in annoyance. "What does it matter?"

"There must be a reason. Think."

She tried to concentrate on the question and not on her queasy stomach or the tossing boat or the slapping waves. "My mother grew them," she said after a moment. "I can remember her making arrangements of them. Even then I liked the bright colors. They're…exotic. A little wild."

He was silent for so long, she wondered if he'd heard her. She looked back at him and found him studying her, the corners of his mouth quirked up in the beginnings of a smile. "Exotic. I can see there's more to you than I expected."

She started to ask what he meant by that, but the engines shut off and seconds later, they bumped against the dock. He stood and offered her his hand. "There. You made it. Once you're back on land, you'll feel fine."

She allowed him to pull her to her feet. Already, her stomach felt more settled. As his hand at her back guided her toward the front of the boat, understanding dawned. She stopped and turned to him. "All those questions about flowers—they were just to distract me, weren't they?"

He shrugged. "Sometimes not thinking about seasickness helps."

"Thank you." She smiled, surprised and pleased to see this softer, gentler side of him. Maybe there was more to Jake than the sarcastic bad boy he played so well.

"You have a nice smile," he said. "You should use it more often."

Was he flirting with her? She wasn't sure if she liked it or not. She pulled her hand from his, the old awkwardness returning. "I...I guess we'd better get off of here."

Laughing and talking, the other couples headed down a shell path toward a lattice-shaded building marked Reception, leaving Jake and Glynna alone. A tall, thin African-American woman with razor-cut hair and a figure-hugging white pantsuit stepped forward and greeted them. "You must be Jake and Glynna," she said, extending her hand. "I'm Marcie Phillips, director of marketing here at La Paloma. Welcome. We're so glad you could join us for our grand opening."

"I'm looking forward to seeing your operation here." Glynna looked around them at the palm-shaded palapas, the rows of colorful sailboats lined up opposite a beach volleyball court and the marble-trimmed swimming pool ringed by lounge chairs filled with sunning couples. "This is quite a setup."

"I've left press kits in your cottage, and of course, I'm available to answer any questions you might have while you're here."

She instructed them to leave their bags on the dock for the porter to bring later, and set off down a path. "I've put you in one of our deluxe cottages," she said. "All of our accommodations are right on the beach and feature private whirlpool tubs and shaded verandas."

Glynna hurried to keep up with Marcie's brisk pace. "Excuse me," she said. "Did you say one cottage?"

Marcie scarcely slowed down. "Of course. It's designed as the perfect couple's getaway. Each has a king-size bed, plus a well-appointed sitting room with a stereo, DVD player—"

"But there are two of us." Glynna put a hand on Marcie's arm, stopping her. "We'll need two cottages."

Marcie looked from Glynna to Jake, frown lines deepening on her forehead. "I thought you understood. This is a couples-only resort. I'm sure I made that quite clear to your editor."

Glynna struggled to keep her voice even. "Jake and I aren't a couple."

Marcie shook her head. "We're completely booked for our grand opening. This is the only cottage we have available."

Glynna looked at Jake. He'd helped her out on the boat. Would he help her now? He raised one eyebrow. "I can share if she can. After all, we're both adults, and it's only for a weekend."

Glynna's stomach dropped to somewhere in the vicinity of her knees. Spend the weekend with sarcastic, sharp-tongued and dangerously sexy Jake Dawson? They'd drive each other crazy within a matter of hours.

"That would be wonderful." Marcie looked relieved. She smiled at Glynna. "Thank you for being so understanding."

She looked up and found Jake's eyes on her. "What do you say?" he asked. "Or are you worried I'll tarnish your virtue?"

Now he'd done it. She had to agree or she'd look like a prude. She held her head up and adopted what she hoped was an air of indifference. "It doesn't matter to me if it doesn't matter to Jake. We'll both be busy working most of the time anyway."

"Great. Your cottage is right over here." Marcie started down the path again, and led them to the last in a row of six. The square whitewashed building had blue shutters, porches on three sides and abundant heart and dove gingerbread trim. "How romantic," Jake leaned forward and growled into Glynna's ear, the rough timbre of his voice sending a jolt through her.

After giving them a brief tour of the three rooms that made up the cottage, Marcie finally left them alone. The porter appeared seconds later and deposited their luggage just inside the door.

Glynna carried her suitcase into the bedroom. Jake followed. "Don't worry," he said. "I won't lay a finger on you. You're not really my type."

She flinched at the remark. Not that she was interested in a man like Jake, but did he have to make a point of telling her she was undesirable?

She opened her suitcase and took out her makeup bag. "I'll take the bed. You can have the sofa."

She started toward the bathroom, but he intercepted her. "No way. I'm a foot taller than you. You take the sofa."

She glared at him, noting not only how tall he was, but how broad his shoulders and chest were. "All right. I'll take the sofa."

"Good." He walked over to the bed and stripped off his shirt in one smooth movement.

She stared, her mouth going dry at the sight of his broad, muscular back. "Wh…what are you doing?" she asked.

"This is the beach. I'm going to change into my swimsuit." He glanced at her. "I suggest you do the same unless you want to really stick out."

He headed for the bathroom, leaving her alone. She opened her suitcase again and took out her most conservative swimsuit—a modest tankini with high-cut legs that suddenly seemed incredibly revealing.

She glanced at the closed bathroom door. Should she change now, or wait until the bathroom was free? What if Jake walked out while she was still undressing?

With trembling fingers, she reached for the zipper on her dress. What if he *did* walk out and find her half-dressed? Would he think her so undesirable then?

She hurriedly stripped and donned the swimsuit, then hung the sundress in the closet and deposited her dirty clothes in a side pocket of her suitcase. The last thing she wanted was to leave her underwear around for Jake to find.

When he emerged from the bathroom, he had a beach towel over one shoulder. He scarcely glanced at her, but went to his bag and took out a digital camera. "I'm going to take a few preliminary shots."

He left without saying goodbye. Glynna stared after him, then sank onto the end of the bed. With Jake gone, the cottage felt too quiet and still. She stared at the painting across from the bed. It depicted a couple walking hand in hand into the sunset. The romantic image mocked her. When was the last time she'd had anything approaching romance in her life? Where was the man who was going to sweep her off her feet and make her forget about work and her father and all the stress in her life?

The men she usually met were either business associates of her father, whom she'd known since she was a toddler, or society playboys whose idea of romance was an expensive dinner at a trendy restaurant, followed by discreet and polite sex. Where were the men who could bring excitement and adventure into her dull existence?

Men like Jake Dawson. The thought sent a tremor through her. Maybe spending the weekend in this cottage with him wasn't such a smart idea. The very fact that he was so different from every other guy she knew acted as a kind of aphrodisiac. How else to explain her sudden attraction to a man who was so clearly not right for her?

She hugged her arms across her chest and frowned at the happy couple in the picture. If Jake knew what she was thinking about him, he'd probably tell her she was out of her mind. "Imagine that," she said out loud. "Something he and I could agree on."

JAKE HAD TO GET out of the cottage before he did something he knew he'd regret. He must have been out of his mind to think he could spend a weekend in close quarters with the ice princess.

Not that she was as cold as he'd thought. In fact, he suspected a hot woman lurked just below the surface. Those were exactly the sort of suspicions he knew would land him in trouble.

The best thing to do, he told himself, was to concentrate on work. Looking at the world through the lens of a camera had given him the perspective to deal with problems in the past. And it had given him goals and hopes and dreams that went beyond the oil fields and cow pastures he'd grown up in. All he had to do was keep looking through that lens, keep taking his pictures, and he'd end up where he wanted to be, in New York, seeing his work on gallery walls and in expensive coffee-table books. He still had a lot to do to get there, and he couldn't let a woman like Glynna McCormick mess with his head and distract him from his goals.

He took some shots of the line of cottages, the flower-filled gardens and the shady palapas. Later he'd view these pictures and decide which scenes and angles would be worth pursuing with his large-format Sinar. He photographed couples lounging by the pool, laughing together on the volleyball court and embracing in the surf. The cynic in him wondered if everyone was really as happy and in love as they looked.

The couple in the ocean parted and began walking down the beach. Jake approached them and introduced himself as a photographer for *Texas Style*. "We're doing a story on the resort and I just took your picture," he said. "Could I ask you a few questions?"

The woman smiled. "We're going to be in a magazine?"

"I can't promise anything, but maybe." He dug in his pocket for the pencil stub and scratch pad he always carried. "Your names?"

"Rich and Emily Spencer," the man said. He was young, midtwenties, with already thinning brown hair and a crooked nose.

"What brings you to La Paloma?" Jake asked.

"We're on our honeymoon." Emily leaned closer to Rich. "Isn't this the most fabulous place?"

"Uh-huh." His attention was distracted by a woman who was walking down the beach toward them. She moved with feline grace along the edge of the waves, her long dark hair blown back over one shoulder, the sun illuminating her skin with a golden glow.

"Do you know her?" Rich asked, following Jake's gaze.

He nodded. "She's the writer I'm working with on this piece."

"Lucky you," Rich said, earning a fierce look from Emily.

"Yeah," Jake mumbled. "I'm lucky all right. Just one lucky dog."

GLYNNA TOLD HERSELF she should be interviewing happy couples, talking to the staff or at least reading through the press kit Marcie had left for her. Instead, the sun and surf had induced an unfamiliar languidness. She strolled the beach, savoring the heat of the sun on her skin and the caress of water against her ankles, inhaling the coconut perfume of suntan lotion and admiring the florescent colors of flowers spilling from planters throughout the grounds. She couldn't remember the last time she'd stopped long enough to enjoy such simple things.

Not that she could totally relax. She still had the article to write, and she still had to deal with Jake. The thought of him sent a rush of envy through her. For all she pretended to disapprove of him, she wished she could borrow a little of his don't-give-a-damn attitude.

She'd held back her own feelings so long, it had become second nature to her. Her father didn't condone "unseemly" behavior. He had taught her that to be a lady and a professional meant remaining cool and unaffected in any situation.

Too late she'd discovered such behavior also meant you often stood alone, unapproachable.

She stopped as she neared a row of beach lounge chairs. A couple shared one chair, their bodies entwined. They looked into one another's eyes, then kissed. They couldn't stop touching each other. She clasped her arms across her chest, staggered by a fierce longing for someone to hold her that way.

As she turned to walk down the beach once more, a heated sensation crept over her, like a warm caress. She looked up and found Jake standing a little way up the beach with a young couple.

His eyes met hers and awareness arced between them, their bodies acknowledging an attraction their minds didn't want to admit. Her first instinct was to turn away, but she fought that and held his gaze. He raised one eyebrow, questioning. She continued to look at him, silently daring him to come to her, to court these dangerous feelings and see what would happen next.

3

JAKE WAS THE FIRST to look away. He turned as if to walk in the opposite direction, but Glynna hurried after him. "Jake, wait up," she called. "I've been looking for you."

He stopped and let her catch up with him, his expression unreadable as he looked out at the ocean. "What have you been doing?" she asked, slightly out of breath.

"I took a few establishing shots of the grounds. Saw some good possibilities for illustrations for the article." He turned to stare at the resort spread out along the shore. "This is sure some place. It has a spa, a sauna, four hot tubs, two swimming pools, a gym, four restaurants, two bars and a karaoke club." He shook his head. "Every luxury money can buy."

"You make that sound like a bad thing."

He looked at her at last, the warmth gone from his eyes. "I don't have anything against money. I just object to the attitude so many wealthy people have that because they have bucks, they deserve special treatment."

"Is that why you don't like me? Because you think I'm some rich bitch?"

To her surprise, he smiled. "Who said I didn't like you?"

She curled her fingers against her palm as she fought the urge to slap him. Not because his remark had offended her, but because he was so annoyingly contrary. Just when she was working up a good head of righteous indignation or anger, he would disarm her by saying something nice.

"I never know what to think of you," she said truthfully.

"And I never know what you're thinking." He held out his hand. "What say we call a truce? We're here in this man-made paradise for the weekend. Why not make the best of it?"

She slipped her hand into his, a curious lightness overtaking her at his touch. She nodded. "You're right. And I…I'm sorry for the way I acted earlier. I'm just…a little tense, I guess." She looked around them, at the sugar-white beach and the aquamarine ocean, the lacy palm trees and the lounging couples. The sun warmed her skin, melting away the tension. Her real life seemed very far away. "Being here has made me realize how much I need to relax."

He continued to hold her hand long after she would have pulled away. "I know just what you need." He strode across the sand, pulling her along with him.

"Wait!" She stumbled, hurrying to keep up with him. "Where are we going?"

"To the bar. We'll have you relaxed in no time."

WHY HADN'T HE noticed before what a great smile she had? Jake sat on a bar stool next to Glynna, watching as she twirled the miniature paper parasol in her glass of rum punch. She had small, even white teeth and full, pink lips. Luscious lips, made for kissing.

He straightened and blinked. Where the hell had that thought come from? He looked down and discovered his own glass was empty. He shoved it across the bar. He'd better slow down, if his mind was taking off in wild directions like that.

She shifted to sit with her back to the bar, facing out toward the ocean. The bar itself was open to the elements on three sides, so that the sea breeze brought the smell of salt and suntan oil and the shouts and cheers from the volleyball game to them. "To think I didn't want to come here," she said.

"Why didn't you want to come?" he asked. Not that he'd jumped at the chance to take the assignment. He had too many other irons in the fire to spend a weekend at the beach.

"I don't usually write fluff pieces like this." She looked at him over the rim of her glass. "And I have so much work to catch up on, and errands and…stuff." She laughed. "Meaningless stuff." She sipped her drink, making long slurping sounds as she drained it. She giggled. "And I thought it wouldn't be fun."

He told himself he shouldn't laugh, but he couldn't hold back the chuckles. This was a different Glynna McCormick than he'd ever seen. Away from the office and out of those severe suits she always wore, she was softer, funnier…and sexy as hell.

He was a fool for agreeing to spend the weekend with her without putting his hands on her. His gaze moved over the curve of her breasts at the neckline of the swimsuit top, to the smooth triangle of thigh showing at the slit of her sarong. She was a woman made for touching, and he was a man not used to denying himself.

If he wasn't already crazy, he was liable to be half-insane before the weekend was over. Maybe he should sleep on the beach....

"Tell me about the nude photos."

The question startled him from his musings. He stared at her. "What nude photos?"

She laughed. "The ones that fell out of your bag at the office the other day." She leaned toward him. "Are you freelancing for *Playboy* or something?"

He coughed. "Yeah, right. If *Playboy* was knocking on my door, I wouldn't need this gig."

"Then what were they for?"

He shifted on the bar stool, picked up his empty glass and set it down again. "It's for a show at a gallery downtown. A series of photos of artistic nudes."

"You mean a gallery showing of just your photos?"

He nodded, watching her out of the corner of his eye. "It's not a big gallery, but if the work sells well, it could lead to bigger things."

"I doubt very many photographers get their own showings. I'm impressed." She opened and closed the parasol, sliding it in and out of her fingers. "It was a beautiful photo. Who was the model?"

"The wife of a friend of mine. He came with her to the shoot and I agreed to give them prints in lieu of a modeling fee." He shrugged. "You do what you have to when you're paying your dues."

"And what are you paying your dues for? I mean, where do you want to go with this?"

"I'd like to go on to exhibit nationally. To be represented in New York, be one of the top names in art photography."

"You have the talent. I guess all you need now is luck." Her voice was breathy, wistful.

He leaned toward her. "What about you? Do you do other writing besides your work for the magazine?"

She shrugged. "I have some investigative pieces I'm working on. But I'm so busy I don't really have time to devote to them."

"If you could do anything, be anything, what would it be?"

"I'd like to go to New York to write for a major magazine there."

"Then why don't you do it? What's stopping you?"

She frowned, and traced her finger through the condensation on the side of her glass. "My father..."

He put his hand on her arm. Her skin was cool and smooth. She looked at him, but didn't move away. "Are you going to let him run your life forever?"

She did jerk away from him then. "You don't know what you're talking about."

"I'm not blind. I see the way you jump every time he says hop." He sat back and reached for his glass, wishing it weren't empty. "You're a grown woman. Why not act like it?"

"Go to hell, and take your opinions with you." She shoved off the bar stool and stalked away, swaying only slightly when she stepped out onto the sand.

Cursing under his breath, he turned from the sight of her and signaled the bartender for another drink. Now he'd done it. Just when he thought they were connecting. Though why should he care? He and Glynna were from two different worlds. His father and grandfather had been oil-field roughnecks who spent their time off in Telephone Road ice houses, drinking beer and playing pool while Glynna's family sat behind desks in clean suits all day, then drank cocktails and munched hors d'oeuvres around the swimming pool in the evenings. She'd had her career gift-wrapped for her the day she graduated from some upper-crust college. She didn't know what it meant to struggle to prove yourself. So why should her opinion of him matter at all?

GLYNNA DRESSED for dinner, but all she really wanted was to take three ibuprofen and crawl under the covers until morning. Why, oh why had she drunk those two rum punches? The sun hadn't even set and already it felt like the morning after.

But her head wasn't the only thing that hurt her. Jake's words had wounded like a dart in her flesh, all the more painful because she knew they were true. Of course she had been letting her father run her life. Anyone would see that on the surface. But did they understand he was all she had? It had been just the two of them since her mother died when she was nine. He'd discouraged relationships with men, even talked her into living at home until two years ago, when she'd insisted on her own place.

So here she was, twenty-six and alone. She'd never done anything her father didn't approve of. For a long time, that had worked for her. She'd made a life for herself, but maybe that wasn't enough anymore.

And now here was Jake, offering opinions she hadn't asked for and imposing all his rough edges on her nice smooth life. Her father disliked Jake, but Jake didn't care. Where others quaked at Gordon McCormick's rages, Jake stood up to him.

She sank onto the edge of the sofa, hands in her lap. There were times when she would have given almost anything for that kind of courage. Not just the backbone to go against her father, but the guts not to feel guilty about it afterwards.

Maybe this weekend was her chance to learn a few things from Jake. A shiver chased down her spine at the thought and she hugged her arms across her stomach, as if trying to hold in the excitement kindling within her.

But the thought had taken root in her and wouldn't let go. No one she knew was on this island. Her father wasn't here this weekend. But Jake was, so why not take advantage of that? Why not indulge in her own fantasies, romantic and otherwise?

Jake said she needed to be her own woman. So why not ask him to help her discover exactly what kind of woman she really was?

JAKE WAS SITTING at the bar when Glynna walked in. He looked up and saw her standing in the doorway and it was as if the temperature in the room rose ten degrees. He tried to look away, to ignore her, but she drew his gaze, like a riptide pulling him under.

Still, he managed to turn his back to her as she drew near. He contemplated signaling the bartender for another beer just as she put her hand on his shoulder,

freezing him. "Come walk with me," she said, the soft murmur of her voice cutting through the bar chatter.

The last thing he needed right now was to go walking off into the darkness with her. He swivelled to face her. "Let's stay here," he said. "I'll buy you a drink."

She glanced around the crowded bar, at the laughing couples with their sunburned faces and umbrella drinks. "No. I need to ask you something. In private."

He shook his head. "That's not a good idea."

"Why not?

He shoved the glass aside, then let his gaze linger on her too long. She was wearing a little strapless dress made of some silky, clingy material, the hot pink-orange of a sunset. She crossed her arms, as if shielding herself from his gaze. "Why not?" she asked again.

"Because I've had a little too much to drink and you look way too good in that dress and I'm liable to do something that will get me slapped."

Her laughter startled him. She reached out and took his hand. "Come on. Let's walk."

He didn't resist, letting her lead him out of the bar, past the lighted swimming pool to the shadowy beach. At the edge of the sand, she slipped off her shoes and, picking up her sandals, took his hand and tugged him toward the edge of the water.

He slowed his pace to match hers, and studied her out of the corner of his eye. Moonlight—or the beers he'd had—softened her features, making her look younger, more vulnerable. "So what did you want to talk about?" he asked.

She wrapped her hand more securely around his, but avoided looking at him, focusing instead on the ocean. "You might not know this, but I've always admired you."

A single barking laugh escaped him. "You have a hell of a way of showing it."

She glanced at him. "I guess I deserve that. But it's true. I'm envious of the way you insist on doing things your way, no matter what other people say. You aren't afraid of my father. There aren't many men he can't intimidate."

"You're right. I didn't know you felt that way." He stopped, and pulled her around to face him. "Why are you telling me now?"

She raised her chin and looked him in the eye. He recognized both determination and fear in her gaze. The fear surprised him. Why would a woman who had everything be afraid of anything? "I want to ask a favor of you this weekend."

"What is that?"

She wet her lips, a provocative, sensuous gesture he felt all the way to his groin. "I want you to pretend that I'm not the Glynna McCormick you think you know. That I'm not Gordon's daughter."

He raised his hand and traced the soft line of her jaw. "Then who are you?"

She cradled her head against his hand. "I'm just a woman. A woman who's tired of doing what everyone expects of me. I want to spend this weekend doing what I want, getting reacquainted with part of myself I've put second for too long."

He stilled, holding his breath. "And what do you want?"

"This." She stood on tiptoe, and put her arms around

his neck, pulling him to her. Her lips were soft against his, the kiss tentative at first, then more assured.

He resisted for the briefest moment, stunned, before instinct and desire took over and he gathered her closer. He shaped her body to his as he deepened the kiss, opening his mouth to taste her fully. She made a breathy, mewling sound that ripped away the last shred of his reserve. He forgot everything but how much he wanted her. Here. Now.

He cupped her bottom, pressing her close against him, savoring her heat against his growing erection. She hooked one leg around him, her gauzy skirt falling back to reveal the pale beauty of her inner thigh. He slid his hand up that silky expanse of flesh, toward the burning center where he wanted to bury himself.

She nipped at the corner of his mouth. "Let's go back to the cottage," she whispered.

The cottage. Like a cold wave splashing over them, the words reminded him of where they were. Why they were here. Who she was.

He pulled away from her, so suddenly that she almost fell. "This is insane," he said.

"Yes, it's insane." She stared at him, out of breath. Flushed. Gorgeous. "That's the whole point. I…I want us to spend this weekend doing all the things we can never do back home. Exploring those fantasies I'm supposed to be writing about."

He took another step back, as if physical distance could break the spell she'd cast over him. "You mean you want us to have sex."

She flushed more, but nodded. "Yes."

"Why? Beyond the obvious reasons that we turn each other on?"

"I think…" She wet her lips again, almost sending him over the edge. "I think a weekend like this, totally indulging myself, will help me understand what it is I really want to do. I know this sounds crazy to someone like you, who's always done exactly what you felt like, but I've been trying to make myself into the person I think I should be for so long I'm not sure I know anymore who I really am."

"And you think a weekend screwing me will do it?" He was deliberately crude, hoping to shock them both back to their senses.

She flinched, but didn't back down. "It's the most radical thing I can think of, so yes." She smiled. "And I think we'd both enjoy it, very much."

Hell yes, he'd enjoy it. And it might even be fun to see the straitlaced ice princess thaw a little. "What happens when we get home?"

She held her hands up, fingers spread wide. "No strings. We go our own ways and no one knows this ever happened."

A weekend of great sex with a gorgeous woman, no strings? "I'd be crazy to say no."

"Then why don't we get started?" She smiled and reached for his hand.

He took it and pulled her toward the path to the cottages, eager now. "It's only fair to warn you." He grinned at her. "I don't intend to stop until the boat pulls up Sunday evening."

4

BACK AT THE COTTAGE, Glynna busied herself lighting candles. The bravado that had led her to make her wild proposition was fading fast, now that she was alone with Jake in this intimate space.

The rustle of fabric against skin disturbed her thoughts. She whirled to see Jake pulling off his shirt. "Wh—what are you doing?" she stammered.

He unfastened the snap of his pants. "I don't know about you, but I prefer to do these things naked."

She clutched the matchbook so tightly it bent in two. "Yes, but...don't you think we ought to talk first?"

"I thought we already talked." He shoved his pants to the floor and stepped out of them. Now he was dressed only in tight black briefs that left little to the imagination. "Or are you having second thoughts?"

"No. Of course not." She sat on the edge of the bed, her legs too wobbly to support her anymore. She glanced at him again. The candlelight burnished his broad shoulders and muscular thighs with gold, and glinted on the dusting of hair across his chest. His nipples were two small brown pebbles against his paler skin, his navel a perfect indentation in his flat stomach.

He walked toward her, moving easily, comfortable in his skin, confident in his sexuality.

He stopped in front of her, the thick ridge of his erection almost at eye level, impossible to ignore. She swallowed, her face burning.

"What's wrong?" he asked.

She raised her head and looked into his eyes, hoping he wouldn't laugh at her. "I…I've never done anything like this before."

The lines around his mouth tightened. "You've never had sex?"

She squeezed her hands into fists. "No. I mean yes, I've had sex. But not…not planned, like this. With someone I don't know very well." She looked toward the double doors leading to the veranda. Was it too late to run away, back to her lonely, safe apartment? But if she did that, things would never be different for her, would they? Her real self would still be trapped somewhere between the roles she played of obedient daughter and conscientious employee.

She raised her eyes to look at Jake again. He watched her, saying nothing, his face calm. Patient. But another emotion flickered in his eyes. Encouragement? For her?

She took a deep breath and went on. "You've had a lot of experience and I…I haven't."

"Are you afraid we won't please each other?" He knelt before her, and put his hands on her thighs. The silk of her dress rustled beneath his fingers as he caressed her through the cloth. "You don't have anything to worry about. Just relax. Do whatever feels good."

He pushed the skirt up a few inches and bent to kiss her knee. "We'll go slow at first. Get used to each other."

His breath was hot, burning its way up her leg as he trailed kisses up the inside of her thigh from her knee to the lacy edge of her underwear. She felt as if she was melting from within, the tension coiling inside of her as his mouth drew closer and closer to the juncture of her thighs.

Her eyes fluttered shut as his mouth closed over the thin silk of her panties. Need built within her, fierce and demanding. It had been so long….

"Do you like the way this makes you feel?" he asked, his mouth still pressed against the silk.

Her reply was more moan than speech, and she felt his lips curve into a smile.

"There's so much more to enjoy," he murmured. He pushed the dress up farther and kissed her stomach, his tongue tickling her navel before climbing the ladder of her ribs to her breasts. He ringed each mound with kisses, painting concentric circles with his tongue, drawing closer and closer to her taut, sensitive nipples.

"Nice." Still kneeling before her, he stripped off her dress and settled his hands on her hips, drawing her closer, until she was straddling his torso, legs spread wide to embrace him, the wet silk of her panties the only barrier between them.

He flicked his tongue across her nipple, and she arched against him, gasping at the waves of desire that washed over her each time he touched her. He suckled first one breast, and then the other, until she was trembling with need, her throbbing sex straining against his pounding heart.

When he raised his head, she cried out and clung to him, but he gently pushed her away. "I'm not going to leave you," he said. "But now it's your turn to get better acquainted with me."

He stood and stripped off his briefs. She stared at his erection, mesmerized by its frank eroticism. No one would call the male member beautiful, yet she couldn't stop staring at it, the tension within her responding to each swaying movement as he walked toward her again.

"Move over so I can lie down beside you."

She did so, hesitating only a moment before slipping out of her panties. She stretched out on the bed and turned to face him, wanting to wrap herself around him and demand he enter her, but holding back.

"What do you want me to do?" she asked.

His sleepy, seductive smile made her heart race. "Touch me," he said. "Wherever you want to touch me."

Hesitant, she put a hand on his shoulder. His skin was warm, the muscles firm beneath her palm. She trailed her fingers down his chest, her nails dragging at the golden hairs, coming to rest on one pebbled nipple.

She bent and kissed it, tongue flicking, lips devouring. He sucked in his breath, and squeezed her shoulder, silently urging her to keep going.

She transferred her attention to his other nipple. He smelled of musk and sweat and warm skin, and tasted slightly salty. She couldn't recall the last time she'd been so close to anyone, and reveled in the contact.

He shifted, wrapping one leg around her and pulling her closer. The tip of his erection pressed against her, demanding entrance. She started to raise her leg to allow him access, then thought better of it and reached down to take him in her hand. He was hot and heavy and holding him like this made her want him all the more. He tried to kiss her, but she turned her head away. "We need a condom," she whispered.

Without a word, he slid off the bed and went into the bathroom. She rolled over onto her back and closed her eyes, savoring the tension in every nerve. The breeze from the ceiling fan caressed her, puckering her nipples, cooling her sex.

She heard foil tearing and opened her eyes to watch Jake sheath himself with the condom. Then he lay beside her. She started to move into his arms, but he held her off. "Maybe we should talk some more," he said, his eyes teasing her.

Laughing, she pushed him down onto his back and straddled him, then wrapped her hand around his shaft and squeezed. The glazed look that came into his eyes thrilled her. "Do you really want to talk?"

He grunted and caressed her hips. "Your body's been talking to mine all day and I like what it's been saying."

She rose up on her knees and guided him into her, sighing as he filled her. She tightened around him and began to move, slowly at first, wanting to savor every delicious sensation radiating through her.

But need soon overtook her, and her movements became more urgent. He reached up to caress her breast, then slid his hand down to her clit. As he fondled and stroked, raw wanting overtook all caution. Bracing her hands on his chest, she rocked over him, each thrust hard and deep, withdrawing almost completely before driving down again.

Her climax was sudden and fierce, exploding within her and reverberating in waves. He followed with a low groan, thrusting up to meet her, shuddering with his release.

She collapsed against him, burying her head in the hollow of his shoulder, holding him tightly as she waited for the waves of sensation to gentle and still.

His hand on her back was heavy and reassuring. She smiled and snuggled closer. To think she had ever disliked him.

Still holding her, he rolled them over until they were on their sides, facing each other. She smiled at him. "That was pretty spectacular."

He smoothed his hand along the dip of her waist. "I think you may have a talent for this."

"I'm betting there's still a few things you can teach me."

"Something tells me you'll be a good pupil." He switched onto his back, away from her. She started to follow him, but resisted. It wouldn't do to get too close. After all, they were only together for the weekend. She shouldn't forget that.

The knowledge made her cold. She sat up and swung her legs over the side of the bed. "Where are you going?" he asked.

"I haven't had dinner. I thought I'd grab something to eat."

"We could order room service." He reached over and stroked her hip. "Ever eat dinner off your lover's body?"

The image the words evoked sent heat curling through her. She shook her head. "I'm going out." She needed to get away from him for a while. To remind herself that this was only an experiment. Temporary. If she stayed with him right now it would be too easy to lose herself in him again. To pretend the feelings he'd kindled in her were real. The sort that lasted forever.

She went into the bathroom and washed off then dressed in shorts and a sleeveless blouse. No underwear, because she didn't want to go back into the bedroom and feel Jake's eyes on her as she searched. Going without felt sexy and decadent, but then, this was a night for that.

When she glanced in the mirror she was startled by the image that confronted of her. Her hair was mussed, her lips slightly swollen, her cheeks flushed. She looked like a woman who was well and truly satisfied. If she had seen herself on the streets, she would have thought she was a woman in love.

But of course, that wasn't the case at all. In lust, maybe, but there was a big difference.

She combed her hair and splashed water on her face, then took a deep breath and opened the door to the bedroom.

The bed was empty. Surprised, she looked around for Jake. The chair where he'd left his clothes was empty, and so was the rest of the cottage. Jake was gone.

JAKE JOGGED ALONG the beach, bare feet pounding against the sand in time to his furiously beating heart. He clenched his hands into fists and ran harder, head down, fighting anger and frustration. What had Glynna meant, walking out on him like that? Had she gotten what she wanted, and that was that? He knew men who acted like that, but a woman?

Could a woman really turn her feelings on and off like that? What had happened between them had been powerful. The kind of sex people fantasize about but rarely experience.

He slowed down, muscles protesting as his feet dragged in the sand. More likely, Glynna was scared. That was it. He doubted Ms. Glynna McCormick had screamed like that in bed with a man more than a few times in her life. If ever. Tonight he'd stripped her bare, both physically and emotionally. A woman like her was bound to be shook up after that.

He stood and looked out at the dark bay. Breakers thundered against the jetty to his left and the distant throb of music from the karaoke club drifted on the night breeze. Hell, he was shook up himself. When she'd taken him in her hand and turned her head away from his kiss, he'd felt something twist inside him, and he'd come dangerously close to pleading with her not to turn away. He'd been relieved to get up to go find a condom, buying time for him to get a hold of himself.

That was it, then. Glynna wasn't dissatisfied with him. She was afraid. And wasn't the whole idea of this weekend to help her get over that fear of her own ideas and emotions? She might have a natural talent for sex, but she needed Jake for the rest. He'd have to find a way to push her past her fear. And he'd be the one to bene-fit. At least this weekend.

He turned back up the beach, headed toward the grill, the only restaurant open at this late hour. She wasn't going to run away from him so easily. The night was young and the weekend short. They had a lot to do. There was one pretty incredible woman inside Glynna, and he couldn't wait to help discover her.

GLYNNA SAT at the grill, idly swirling a French fry through a pool of ketchup, wondering how she could go from feeling fantastic one moment and more alone and uncertain than ever the next.

Was Jake angry with her for leaving him so quickly after their lovemaking? Was that why he'd left? Was she wrong to have pulled away from him?

What did it matter what he thought? Why was she worrying about doing what he wanted her to do when the whole point of this weekend was supposed to be for her to discover what *she* wanted—really wanted.

Back there in the cottage, what she'd craved was to stay with him. She wanted to feel his arms around her, holding her close and then, after a while, to make love again. They'd go slowly this time, savoring each touch and response. She wanted to know that for that brief span of time at least, she could be anything, do anything, and no one would object.

Instead, she'd given in to guilt and fear and run away. Despite the incredible experience in Jake's arms, nothing had really changed inside her.

"Is the food really that bad?"

She jumped as Jake reached around her and snagged a French fry from her plate. He chewed, a thoughtful look on his face. "Not bad. But cold." He slid onto the stool beside her.

"Where have you been?" she asked.

"I went running on the beach." He glanced at her. "I needed to get away and think."

"Yeah." She could understand that. "Me, too." She pushed her plate away and took a sip from her glass of diet soda. "What did you decide?"

He swivelled to face her. "I've pretty much made it my policy to say what I think about things. Some people don't like it, but they don't have to worry about me lying to them, either."

She eyed him warily. What was he getting at? "It's one of the things I admire about you. So?"

He put his elbow on the counter and leaned toward her. "So you have to shoot straight with me, too. Why did you run out on me just now?"

Her stomach knotted. Talking about her feelings was not something she was good at. In fact, she avoided it whenever possible. "You know, I said I wanted to have sex with you. Not bare my soul."

"You said you wanted to find out what kind of woman you really are." He took her hand and laid it in his, palm up, as if he was about to tell her fortune. "Lesson number one—a lot of sex takes place inside a person's head. And I want to know what's going on in yours. Why did you run out?"

She tried to pull her hand away, but his fingers encircled her wrist, trapping her. His gaze on her was steady. Relentless. She was going to have to answer his question. She took a deep breath. "I think I was a little overwhelmed by what happened. It wasn't what I expected."

He raised one eyebrow. "I hope that means it was better than you expected."

She nodded, one quick jerk of her head. "Oh, yeah. Better. And…different."

With his forefinger, he traced her lifeline, coming to rest at her pulse. "It was pretty intense." His eyes met hers again. "I can't say that's happened to me very often."

"It's never happened to me before. I…I don't know what it means."

"It could be that it's been a while for both of us, and that intensified the experience. Or it could mean that we're particularly well-matched, physically." He smiled, his eyes crinkling at the corners. "Who would have guessed it?"

She flushed. "We aren't that much alike, are we?"

"But maybe more than you give yourself credit for."

His words startled her into smiling. "You can't be serious. We're nothing alike."

He shrugged. "Think about it. We're both driven. Ambitious. We don't have patience with incompetence."

She studied his long hair, faded T-shirt and baggy shorts. He was sexy in a just-rolled-out-of-bed way, but he was completely unlike any man she'd ever dated. She couldn't imagine them being truly compatible. "We live completely different kinds of lives," she said.

"I'm not likely to forget that." His gaze took in her silk shirt and designer shorts. "But this weekend, none of that matters, does it?" He released her hand. "This weekend is about doing what feels good. About taking that intensity and running with it." He stroked her cheek with one finger. "About learning to loosen up and let go."

She nodded. "Yes." At least for this weekend she had to stop listening to what her head told her to do, and pay more attention to her heart. She took a deep breath and looked him in the eye. "So what now?"

He sat back and studied her. "I think I want to photograph you."

She started to laugh, but the seriousness in his eyes stopped her. "Why would you want to do that?"

"I want to photograph you naked."

The passion in his eyes warmed her, as did the blush that rose to her cheeks once more. "I don't think—"

His hand on her thigh stopped her. "Don't think about it now. We'll talk later. Before the weekend is over." He stood and held out his hand. "Come on. Let's go for a walk."

"Where are we going?" She slid off the stool and put her hand in his.

"Someplace where we can be alone." He smiled down at her, mischief in his eyes. "Time for lesson number two."

5

THEY WALKED along the beach, not speaking. Jake was lost in thought, scarcely aware of Glynna's hand in his or the waves washing over their feet. The idea to photograph her had just come to him, but the more he thought about it, the more intrigued he was. She had a physical beauty that would translate well to film—the trick would be capturing both the outer hardness and inner vulnerability of her personality.

"Where are we going?" she asked again.

Her question pulled him away from puzzling over lighting and setting and all the variables a good photograph entails, back to the woman herself. He glanced at her. The wind had tangled her hair and moonlight silvered her skin. How had he ever thought she was cold? "I'm not sure. But I'll know it when I see it." He'd decided earlier that a woman who was always so worried about what others thought of her—or at least what her father thought—needed to be challenged to flaunt convention. Now he had to figure out how to do that.

The music from the karaoke club was closer now. According to the resort brochure, after midnight it became a dance club, with an outdoor dance floor overlooking the ocean. "Let's go to the club," he said, heading in that direction.

She lagged behind. "I don't want to dance."

He grinned. "You'll like this kind of dancing. I promise."

Instead of leading her to the club directly, he took her to the beach below the dance patio. Stone steps led up to the patio itself, and a row of coconut palms lined the stone wall that separated it from the beach. If he remembered correctly… Yes, there it was. A hammock swung between two of the palms, just on the edge of the light spilling from the dance floor.

He led her to the hammock. "What are you doing?" she asked.

"I thought this would be a nice place for a little private dancing."

She looked up, a worried frown wrinkling her normally smooth brow. Music pounded overhead, mixed with laughter, the clink of glasses and the shuffling of dancing couples. "What do you mean?"

He pulled her into his arms, tight against his erection, so she'd have no doubt of his feelings. "Have you ever made love in a public place before?"

"No!"

She tried to pull away, but he held her close, studying her face to gauge her reaction to his words. "It can be very exciting." He trailed one finger along her collarbone, down around the curve of her breast. Her lips parted and she let out a soft sigh. "Knowing that at any moment, you might be caught. Someone might hear you." He kissed her neck and she arched against him.

She smelled of vanilla and spice and herbal shampoo. "Someone might see you."

"I don't think this is a good idea," she murmured.

"Why not? It's not all that public." He raised his head and looked around them. "It's relatively dark under here. No one can really see us. And the music's loud. They won't hear us. Unless you scream." He nibbled her neck. "You like to scream when you come, don't you? And I intend to make you come. Long and hard."

"Jake, I…"

He pulled back enough to look her in the eye. "You said you wanted to find out about yourself. You do that by taking chances, by doing things you've never done before."

She glanced over his shoulder, out onto the empty beach. "If anyone did see us, they wouldn't know who we were, would they?"

"They'd think we were one more honeymoon couple, overcome by passion." He raked his thumb over her nipple. It hardened at his touch.

"All right." She gave him a tentative smile. "I'll play."

The knowledge that she'd overcome her natural reluctance stirred him. He kissed her, hard and deep, his tongue plunging and withdrawing in frank imitation of what he would do with her later. She responded with surprising ardor, pressing against him, her tongue teasing his. While his mouth made love to hers, he caressed her breasts. The silk of her shirt slid beneath his hand, heightening sensation. Her moan cut through him as he flicked his thumb across her distended nipples.

"Here. Sit down." He nudged her back until she half

sat, half fell into the hammock. It swung forward, bumping against him, and she wrapped her legs around him, bringing his erection flush between her spread legs.

Before he could move back, she reached down and shaped her hand to him. "I love it that you're so hard already," she said, the whispered words making him harder still.

Determined to maintain control of the situation, he pushed her hand away and took her shirt in both hands and shoved it up over her breasts. Her naked skin was pale in the dim light, her nipples small dark points. At the first touch of his lips on her, she cried out, then clamped her hand over her mouth to muffle the cry. "That's right," he whispered against her breast. "Someone might hear us."

She whimpered and ground against him. The friction was driving him mad and he reached down to unzip his shorts. Her hand on his stopped him. "Let me."

He wanted to say no, that he was in charge of this "lesson," but her eyes locked to his convinced him giving up this little bit of command would be worth it. With agonizing slowness, she lowered the zipper, letting her thumb trail the hard ridge of his cock. Dropping her gaze to his crotch, she pulled back his briefs, and touched the spot of wetness forming at the tip of his penis. He sucked in his breath as she took one finger and spread the moisture around the head. Her touch sent electric shocks of sensation through him, and he had to lock his knees to keep standing. If he wasn't careful, this was all going to be over in a hurry.

Partly to distract her, and partly to distract himself,

he slipped two fingers underneath the crotch of her shorts. She was wet and naked under there, the twin sensations loosening his control another notch. With a groan, he shoved her hand away from him, and buried his fingers in her slick heat. She gripped him, the muscles in her thighs tightening, her back flexing. "That feels so good," she hissed. "Please don't stop."

"Baby, I don't intend to stop." He parted her folds with his thumb and began to stroke her, gently at first, then more firmly. His fingers found her G-spot and began to stroke there, as well. She coiled around him, tension building, and began to pant with breathy moans.

He looked at her. Her head was thrown back, her hair a wild tumble down her back. Her lips, still swollen from his kisses, were parted, her eyes closed, lacy lashes dark against her pale face. She was gorgeous in a way she'd never been before, wild and primal, unbound by inhibition or convention. The sight of her transformed by lust and need fed his own desire.

He lowered his head to her breast once more and had no sooner taken her in his mouth again before she exploded beneath him. Her muscles gripped him and she bit his shoulder to keep from crying out as she shook with the force of her climax. He threw both arms around her and held her close, rocking her, stroking her back.

After a while, her breathing slowed, and she eased back against the hammock and looked up at him. "How come sex has never been like this before?" she asked.

She sounded so astonished, he didn't know whether to laugh or be angry. "Maybe you haven't been with the right guy," he said.

Her gaze drifted down, to the open front of his shorts, and she smiled. "Now it's your turn." She sat up, feet dragging in the sand, and swung the hammock back and forth, bumping against his legs. "This could be interesting."

He grasped her hips to still her. "I think you need to take your shorts off."

He expected her to object, to protest she couldn't get naked when they were practically in public, but eyes locked to his, she stripped the shorts off in one movement and dropped them in the sand. "Your turn," she repeated.

He discarded shorts and briefs, though he felt a little silly with the breeze blowing across his naked butt. Anyone walking by would have no doubt about what was going on in the shadows when they spotted his pale cheeks glowing in the moonlight.

She reached around and cupped his bottom. "You have a very nice butt. I've noticed it before. Especially when you wear your motorcycle leathers."

"Oh, so you've been lusting after me before now?" The thought pleased him.

"I may be a little repressed, but I'm not dead."

"I don't think you're all that repressed, either." He leaned forward, nudging the tip of his penis against her opening. He was anxious to be in her now.

She smiled up at him. "I guess I'm not, am I?" She pushed back with one foot, swinging out of his reach, then poised there, leaning toward him. "Something's missing here."

"Do you mean a condom? I've got one in my pocket."

He started to reach down for his shorts, but she stopped him, one hand wrapped around his cock.

"I was thinking we needed a little more…lubrication." With that, she bent and took him into her mouth. He let out a low groan and clutched her shoulders as her lips and tongue wrapped around him. She licked and suckled, her touch light, then stronger, keeping him teetering on the edge. He gritted his teeth and dug his fingers into her. Should he hold back, or let himself go?

She raised her head and through his glazed vision, he was aware of her smiling at him. "I think we're ready for that condom now."

She took the packet from his stiffened fingers and opened it. He almost lost it when she rolled the rubber on him, but somehow maintained control. Then she lay back and wrapped her thighs around him. "Let's see how this hammock works."

Sinking into her was sheer heaven. She tightened around him, hot and wet, and he thrust forward, rocking the hammock. With little effort, they fell into a steady rhythm of thrust and sway, a tantalizing dance in time to the music which throbbed overhead. He closed his eyes and gave himself up to sensation: the pulsing music, the smell of sand and saltwater and sex, the exquisite sensation of Glynna clenching him, holding and releasing him, desire building, as he thrust faster, deeper…

He kept thrusting as his climax swept through him, riding the waves up and over. When he collapsed on the hammock at last, he was completely spent. Glynna enveloped him with her arms and legs and held him, the hammock swaying gently. He rested his head against her breast, eyes closed, and breathed in the sweet scent of her. He couldn't remember ever being so sated, so content. The thought came to him that if he could capture the emotion of this instant on film, he would be a true genius. But then, a perfect moment like this was as fleeting as the few seconds at certain times of year when the light was exactly right to make a perfect photo. Neither the light nor the moment was meant to last. The only thing he could do was enjoy them while they were here, and not mourn them when they were gone.

GLYNNA WOKE the next morning, uncharacteristically stiff. She smiled as she stretched. Obviously, her body wasn't used to being so…active. Still smiling, she rolled over and reached for Jake. She had a few ideas for waking him….

But the place beside her was empty. She sat up and looked around, a sinking feeling in the pit of her stomach. Had he walked out on her again?

The sound of running water registered and she looked toward the closed bathroom door. Of course, he was in the shower. Should she sneak in and surprise him? She was trying to convince herself to get out of bed and do so when the water shut off. So she lay back down and waited.

In a few minutes, the bathroom door opened and Jake emerged, toweling his hair. He was dressed in swim trunks, his torso still wet and gleaming. She let her gaze drift over him, and raised her eyebrows at the sight of a purpling mark on his right shoulder. "What's that on your shoulder?" she asked.

He glanced at the bruise and grinned. "It's where you bit me last night."

She blushed, remembering those wild moments in the hammock. "I did that?"

"Yeah. You were pretty incredible."

And he had been awesome. She looked away, afraid of what he might read in the look on her face. "What are you going to do today?"

"I'm going to take some interior shots—rooms, the bar, things like that. Someone from the resort is supposed to show me around at ten." He tossed the towel onto a chair. "What about you?"

Her preference was to stay in bed with him all day, but they were here on assignment, after all. "I'd better get started with my interviews." She closed her eyes and stretched her arms overhead, arching her back. "Then I might sun by the pool for a while." She seldom took time to relax and do nothing, but this morning the idea appealed to her.

She opened her eyes and caught Jake watching her. The naked desire in his eyes thrilled her. "Did you mean what you said last night, about photographing me?"

He nodded and sat on the edge of the bed. "You saw the work I do— I pose the models so that the emphasis is on their bodies, not their faces. No one would have to know who you are."

She thought of the woman in the photo she'd seen, how beautiful and erotic she'd looked. Jake made her feel that way, but could he really capture that on film? "I'll think about it."

"And I'll be thinking about you today." He raised her

hand to his lips and gave her a look that sent fire curling through her. She leaned toward him. "Maybe you should come back to bed."

He glanced at the clock and shook his head. "You don't know how much I'd like that, but it's almost ten now."

"All right then." Who was she to chide someone about putting work first? But part of her wished he would stay, all the same.

When he was gone, she dressed in swimsuit and cover-up, stowed her notebook and tape recorder in a tote bag and headed for the beach. She ate breakfast at the beach grill, surrounded by cheerful couples. Sitting by herself, she was aware of people watching her. A single person in a place like this couldn't be inconspicuous. She wished Jake had had time to have breakfast with her. One of the surprising things about this weekend had been finding out that he was good company. It made her wonder who else in her life she was misjudging.

Marcie, looking chic in a blue silk sheath and strappy gold sandals, crossed the patio. When she spotted Glynna, she veered off course and headed for her. "How is everything going?" she asked. "Are you enjoying your stay at La Paloma?"

"Yes. It's been very pleasant." The word didn't begin to convey how much she'd been enjoying herself, but the resort had little enough to do with that.

Marcie slid onto the stool next to her. "So what did you do last night?"

"Last night?" She picked up her fork and examined it. "Um, last night I went to the dance club." She smiled, remembering the very private dancing she and Jake had shared.

"I hope you'll take advantage of some of our other amenities while you're here," Marcie said. "We have a wonderful spa. And if you're interested in arts and crafts, there are pottery and watercolor classes this afternoon. Oh, and don't forget the body painting and couples massage classes. Those would be interesting to include in your article."

"Body painting and couples massage?" Glynna wrote these in her notebook. "Yes. Those do sound…interesting." She thought of massaging Jake's body and sparks sizzled through her. What was he doing right now? She looked up, hoping to spot him in the crowd around the pool or on the beach.

"Is there anything else I can do for you?" Marcie's question reminded Glynna that she was supposed to be working. She took out the tape recorder and laid it on the table. "Do you have time to answer a few questions for me about the resort?"

"Of course. I'd be happy to."

She spent the next half hour talking to Marcie about the history of La Paloma and its philosophy. "Your brochure says you 'cater to every couple's romantic fantasies' but what does that mean, exactly?" she asked.

Marcie smiled and trailed one scarlet-tipped nail along the edge of the bar. "We try to make this a world apart, where couples don't have to worry about everyday concerns like bills and jobs. You'll notice we have very few clocks here, and no newspapers or news magazines. We try to give couples all the things they need but don't usually have—time alone, lots of private nooks and romantic places, games that encourage love play."

"So it's all about sex."

Marcie shook her head. "Not *all* about sex, but sex is important to a relationship, wouldn't you agree? Shared intimacy—revealing yourself both physically and emotionally to your partner—is the foundation for a strong bond. For honeymooners, this is their time to find out about each other. For couples who have been together longer, we give them the chance to rediscover all they love about each other."

"But body painting and couples massage?" Glynna raised one eyebrow in question.

Marcie's smile broadened. "Unlike many other cultures, our society emphasizes work and seriousness over play and fun. We want couples to learn to play together here and hope they will carry that sense of fun with them into their everyday world." She leaned toward Glynna, her tone confiding. "Don't tell me the thought of slathering your lover's body with fruit-flavored paint and licking it off doesn't do something for you. And who knows? Later, when you're sitting in some boring meeting, that wonderful fantasy may be what gets you through the day without snapping an obnoxious co-worker's head off."

Glynna clenched her thighs together and shifted on the stool, tension building between her legs as she imagined licking her way up Jake's muscular chest. *Have you ever eaten off your lover's body?* he'd asked last night.

She wet her lips. "I see what you mean." She shut off the recorder and gathered her notebook. "If you don't mind, I'd like to talk to some of the couples here about their experiences at La Paloma." And with any luck, she'd find a certain sexy photographer and suggest they indulge in a little "love play" of their own.

6

JAKE SPENT the morning photographing the interior of honeymoon cottages, and restaurants and bars. They were shots that could have graced any advertising brochure, most of which he wouldn't use. Some of them would run as small "thumbnails" along the margins of the article copy, or a shot of the empty bar might run inset in a shot of the same space full of partying couples. The lion's share of the article's illustrations would be taken out from under the watchful eye of the resort official who shepherded him around this morning. But it was part of the job, pleasing the people who had invited him and, despite his reputation for brashness, he could play the polite game when he had to.

Five rolls of film later, he was free of his handler at last. He gathered his gear and headed for the pool. Glynna had said something about catching some sun. With any luck, he'd find her and persuade her to come back to the room. He got hard thinking about seeing her naked again. He wanted to prove to himself that last night hadn't been just a fluke, the product of too much alcohol and too long a period of abstinence. Was it really possible that a woman he'd dubbed "Ice Princess" had set him afire that way?

At poolside, he was hailed by a woman in the water. "Hey, Jake. Hello!" He recognized Emily Spencer.

Her husband, Rich, swam up beside her. "Still taking pictures for your article?" he asked.

No, I just carry the camera as a prop to pick up women. He bit back the sarcasm and settled for a world-weary attitude. "That's me. Stuck in paradise, having to work."

Rich hauled himself up onto the side of the pool in front of two lounge chairs occupied by another young couple. "These are our friends, Eddie and Karla Davies."

Karla smiled and waved, while Eddie reached out to shake Jake's hand. "Good to meet you."

Emily joined her husband on the side of the pool. "Would you take a picture of the four of us?" she asked. "We're all here on our honeymoon."

You and a hundred others, Jake thought. But he was in a good mood. "Why not?" He motioned toward Karla and Eddie. "Sit up there on the edge of the chair." It was a waste of film, but he would play along.

The two couples gathered in close, the women in front, the men crouched behind them. "Wait," Eddie cried. "We have to toast!" He leaned over and snatched a neon-colored drink off the table. The others grabbed their own glasses and raised them high. "To La Paloma," Eddie said.

Jake grinned. Through the viewfinder, the shot didn't look so bad. The sand castle structure of the main building rose behind the four happy people, who were all young and in love, and obviously having the time of their lives. This might work after all.

He took several shots, then lowered the camera and thanked them. "I'll let you know if there's anything we can use in the magazine," he said. He sat on the edge of an empty lounger to change film, the camera stuck inside his bag to protect it from the bright sun. He worked by touch, his fingers deftly going through motions they'd made a thousand times. "So what made you decide to come to La Paloma?" he asked Eddie. He'd posed the same question to half a dozen other couples so far, and had come to expect the same answer.

"It's so romantic," Karla said. Just as the female half of every other couple had said.

"But what makes it so romantic?" he asked. The usual answer had something to do with the beach, or palm trees or the cottages, but Karla surprised him.

"It's so different from our real life," she said. "No deadlines, no worries. Since everything's paid in advance, you don't even have to figure the tip at dinner or wonder if you can afford another cocktail." She sipped her drink. "Everyone here is catering to you—and let's face it, that's not real life."

"It's a chance to indulge yourself," Eddie added. "To do things you wouldn't normally do, whether it's singing karaoke or getting a little kinky in the bedroom."

"Eddie!" His wife blushed and swatted at him.

Jake laughed. "So what have you done here that's fun? Besides the kinky sex."

Eddie waggled his eyebrows. "What's more fun than that?"

"Seriously, this place is all about sex." Rich joined the conversation. "Did you know they have private hot tubs for two in the gardens? And how many places can you order oysters and something called a ginseng love potion on the room service menu?"

"All right. You've convinced me." Jake zipped up his camera bag and slung it over his shoulder. They'd also given him an idea for the illustrations for Glynna's article. His theme would be sexual fantasy. Hot and steamy, within the bounds of decency. Shadows and artistic angles could accomplish a lot in that respect. He grinned. This was going to be more fun than he'd anticipated.

He said goodbye to the two couples and moved on around the pool. On the other side of the diving board, he spotted Glynna. She was lounging in a chair, talking with another woman. He stopped ten feet away, enjoying the chance to admire her openly.

She looked hot in a pink bikini and sunglasses, a beaded bracelet around her left ankle. His fingers ached to hold the camera again, to photograph her. He'd have to find some way to convince her to let him do it this weekend. He wanted to see her through the lens with the eye of a lover. He'd shoot her after they'd had sex, and capture that sleepy, sated expression.

The other woman left and Glynna looked up and caught him staring at her. Their eyes locked, but he made no move to approach her. Not yet. He wanted to see what she'd do, with him standing here, blatantly undressing her with his eyes.

He wished she'd take the damn sunglasses off, though, so he could see her expressions. Instead, she leaned over and took a tube of sunblock from her bag. She squeezed some onto her leg and began rubbing it in, smoothing it up her thighs in a circular motion, her fingers lightly brushing her crotch. He sucked in his breath, mesmerized by her movements.

She rubbed more lotion on her stomach, and across her chest, fingers dipping into her cleavage, smoothing along the edge of her bikini top. Her nipples were hard, clearly outlined against the thin fabric of the swimsuit. He remembered how 'she'd moaned last night when he'd flicked his tongue across those sensitive tips. He wanted to go to her, to drag her off that lounger and back to their room, but he was painfully hard. He couldn't walk past all these people with his arousal so obvious. He needed to give himself time to cool off.

If she looked at him at all, the sunglasses hid her glance. She returned the sunblock to her bag and wiped her hands on her towel, then turned her attention to a plate of fruit on the table beside her. She selected a slice of mango and bit into it, juice running from the corners of her mouth. She sucked and licked at the pulpy fruit, teeth scraping at the peel, tongue lashing out to capture dripping juice. He gritted his teeth, his cock throbbing. Did she have any idea what she was doing to him?

Mango done, she selected a strawberry, but instead of popping it in her mouth right away, she circled it with her tongue, licking, then nibbling at the sweet red flesh. He was sure she was watching him now. She smiled, and sucked in the last of the berry, then blew him a kiss.

He snatched a towel from an empty lounge chair and knotted it around his waist, then strode toward her, moving as fast as he could in his condition. "Having fun?" he asked when he stood over her.

She smiled, a seductive curve of lips still wet with fruit juice. "Oh, yes."

"Just remember. Paybacks are hell."

"I can't wait to see what you have in mind."

He grabbed her hand and tried to pull her off the lounge chair, but she resisted. "What time is it?" she asked.

Annoyed, he glanced at his watch. "It's almost one. Why?"

She stood and gathered her belongings. "We'd better hurry or we'll be late."

"Late for what?"

"Our class." She stuffed her towel into her bag.

"What class? I'm not interested in any damn class." All he was interested in was getting her into bed again.

She smiled. "I think you'll be interested in this one."

"What is it?"

She slung her tote over one shoulder and faced him. "Couples body painting." She trailed a finger down his chest. "You paint a design on, and then you lick it off."

"Uh-huh." The word emerged as a grunt. He cleared his throat. "And we're going to do this is front of other people?"

She laughed. "I thought you got off on that."

Right. Except that in his current state, it wasn't going to take him long to "get off" at all.

Now that she and Jake were actually in the meeting room where the body painting class was scheduled, Glynna wondered if she was really as brave as she'd pretended to be back there by the pool. She looked around at the other eight couples who lounged on beanbag chairs or oversize pillows on the carpeted floor. Subtle teasing by the pool had been one thing; could she really get physical with Jake in front of all these strangers?

"All right everyone. Looks like we're ready to begin." The instructor, a cheerful dreadlocked blonde named Reyna, motioned them all to gather round. "I want each couple to take a set of paints and make yourselves comfortable."

She began passing out what looked like children's watercolor paint trays, each slot in the tray filled with a dab of a brightly colored paste. Jake dipped his little finger in a glob of purple, then stuck it in his mouth.

"How does it taste?" Glynna asked.

"Not bad. Sort of…grape." He winked at her. "Tastes better on you, I'll bet."

She flushed and concentrated on finding a comfortable position on the beanbag they shared.

"You all remember how to fingerpaint, right?" Reyna asked. "That's what we're going to do today, but your partner's body is your canvas. Decorate it however you like. I want you to get as creative as you dare, and have fun."

Nervous giggles swept the room. Reyna laughed. "Remember, there are no rules. Well, only one. The body paints are edible, so if you make a mistake, we encourage you to erase your work and start over!"

"I'll go first." Before Glynna could protest, Jake snatched the paint tray from her. He studied the selection of colors, then leaned back to look at Glynna. The intensity of his gaze made her nervous. "What are you plotting?" she asked.

"What makes you think I'm plotting something?"

His smile was anything but innocent. He scooped up a fingerful of red paint and drew a line down her breastbone, stopping at the center tie of her bikini.

"What are you doing?"

"You'll see." He selected same green and began sketching in lacy fronds.

"Is that a palm tree?" she asked.

"A coconut palm." He squeezed one of the "coconuts" and she swatted at him.

"What's this painting supposed to be, anyway?"

"A surprise." He selected blue paint and drew a curving, dashed line from the base of the palm tree across her stomach.

The paint felt slick and cool as he stroked it on, warming as it melted into her skin. His touch was light, skimming over her flesh in a way that made her long for more. Her nipples tightened and pressed against the thin fabric of her top, and excitement built up within her.

"Close your eyes," he said. "I want this to be a surprise."

Reluctantly, she did as he asked, and tried to relax against the beanbag. Whispering and muffled laughter from the other couples drifted to her, and the fruity scents of the paints mingled with the coconut aroma of suntan oil for a tropical salad effect.

He added another series of short, smooth strokes beneath her breasts, down her ribs to her stomach. Then he moved away.

She opened her eyes and found him sitting back on his heels, studying his work.

"Can I see?" she asked.

He shook his head. "Not yet. This part's not right."

Leaning down, he began to lick off the last section of his work.

She gasped as his tongue swept across her, hot and velvet-soft. He circled her navel, then stroked along the edge of her bikini bottoms, setting up an insistent throbbing between her legs.

She jumped as his tongue slipped beneath the thin fabric, tantalizing inches away from her aching sex. "What are you doing?" she gasped.

"Wishing I had a longer tongue," came the muffled answer.

"Jake, we're in a public place!" She tried to slide down the chair, out of his reach, but he pinned her with one hand. His tongue continued to move, stroking the top of her mons, driving her to distraction.

She tried to maintain a calm expression, though she was anything but. A glance around her told her no one was looking their way. Everyone seemed too interested in their own art projects.

"All right. I hope everyone is ready to show off your work." Reyna stood and commanded their attention once more.

Jake raised his head and released Glynna. He wiped his mouth and grinned. "Paybacks are hell, aren't they?"

She meant to glare at him, but one look at him, a smear of blue paint like a cartoon moustache above his lips, and she was fighting laughter instead.

"Who wants to be the first to show off their work?" Reyna asked.

A beefy blond man raised his hand. "We'll go first." He stood and helped his wife to her feet. He'd adorned the petite redhead top to bottom with colorful graffiti. From where she was sitting, Glynna could make out the words "Dig it!" "Far out" and "Sock it to me!"

"She's the chick from that old show, *Laugh-In*," someone said.

"Goldie Hawn," someone else supplied the name.

They all laughed and applauded. "Who's next?" Reyna asked.

"We are."

Glynna gasped as Jake hauled her to her feet. "Here we have a very special treasure map," he said.

Glynna stared into the wall of mirrors and was startled to find a credible rendition of a pirate's treasure map, complete with palm tree, ocean waves, a treasure chest and an arrow pointing toward her crotch, with the inscription *Dig Here*. She shook her head, joining in the laughter of those around them.

"Looks a little smeared around her stomach," one man said.

Jake coughed. "Yeah, well…I had to erase."

Glynna sank back to the beanbag as fresh laughter exploded around them. "Very funny," she muttered to Jake.

"I thought it was amusing." He winked at her. "You make a good canvas."

She allowed a smile to break through. "I never knew you were so artistic."

"It takes an illustrator's eye to be good with a camera, don't you think?"

She nodded. Of course Jake was an artist. One look at his photos and anyone could tell.

A few other couples showed off their work. One

young woman had painted her husband in green and brown camouflage, while another couple had decided to work on each other at the same time, labeling various body parts with descriptive adjectives in bright colors.

When there were no more volunteers to show off their work, Reyna asked for a round of applause for them all. "That's all the time we have for this class," she said. "But you're welcome to take the paints back to your cottages and experiment on your own. Have fun."

Glynna picked up the paint tray and gave him a meaningful look. "Does this mean it's my turn now?"

"In a minute." He turned away from her and headed across the room, stopping the graffiti and camouflage couples at the door. "I'd like to get your pictures for the article we're doing for *Texas Style*."

Within five minutes, Glynna was sure Jake had forgotten she was even in the room. He was too busy setting up his camera, positioning his subjects, and adjusting the window shades to regulate the light.

The drying paint on her skin itched, and her stomach growled, her late breakfast a distant memory. She looked down at the paint tray in her hand. The paints were beginning to dry, too. By the time Jake finished his work, they'd be useless.

She set them aside, then slipped on her cover-up and left the room. She was disappointed, but she couldn't be angry at Jake. She of all people understood how important his work was to him. Didn't she feel the same way about her writing?

Still, she didn't like being reminded that the fantasy she'd set out to create this weekend didn't mix well with the reality of her and Jake's everyday lives. She'd promised him she'd make no claims on him after Sunday and, of course, that was the way it had to be. Too bad there wasn't a way to make at least a little of the fantasy last.

7

IT WAS AFTER DARK when Jake returned to the cottage.
He'd spent the rest of the day shooting for the piece.
New ideas came fast and furious and he had to capture
them while inspiration was fresh. He half expected to
find the door locked. Glynna would be pissed. He'd
seen it before—women resented him putting work first.
They said they were attracted to him because he was talented and ambitious, as long as that talent and ambition
didn't take away attention from them.

Yeah, well, he'd handled it before. Glynna of all people knew she didn't have any hold on him. Where did
she get off thinking she had any right to be angry?

The doorknob turned easily in his hand. Cautiously,
he stepped into the darkened living room. He set down
his camera bag. "Glynna?"

"I'm back here."

He followed her voice into the bedroom. Reading
lamps cast soft pools of light around the bed. She was
stretched out on top of the sheets, a short, filmy negligee
leaving more of her bare than it covered. Her skin glowed
in the soft light and her hair hung loose around her shoulders. His anger evaporated, replaced by renewed desire.

He wanted to go to her and gather her in his arms, but he played it cool, trying to read her. "What did you do all afternoon?" he asked, stepping into the room.

"I had a massage at the spa." She stretched her arms overhead, breasts thrust forward. He saw the shadow of her nipples beneath the filmy fabric and his mouth went dry. "It was wonderful."

"Yeah." He wanted to massage her, to touch every inch of her.

"Then I came back here and got some work done on the article. What about you? Did you get some good pictures?"

"Yeah, I did." He sat on the edge of the bed, still wary, waiting for her to lash out at him for walking out on her like that. Looking at her now, he wondered if he hadn't been a little crazy to do so.

"So tell me about them." She sat up, cross-legged. He had trouble keeping his eyes off the shadowed valley between her legs. Was she wearing any underwear? "What did you shoot?" she prompted.

"Oh." He shifted his gaze to her face. Her eyes were calm; she seemed genuinely interested. "I got some great shots of the body painting. I had the couples pose painting each other. Then I got the idea to shoot them in the ocean, washing off the paint." He told her how he'd focused the camera not on faces, but on body parts: a man's hand sweeping across a woman's thigh, water droplets clinging to a shapely stomach and diamond-studded belly ring, a wife kissing her husband's shoulder as a wave arched over them.

"They sound gorgeous. Very sexy."

"That's the idea." He glanced around them, at the plush furnishings and romantic lighting. "This place is all about sex and I wanted photos that would really show that."

She shook her head. "My father is going to faint when he sees them."

Yeah, the old man would blow a fuse. Jake raised his chin, defiant. "The readers will love it."

"I love it." She smiled. "And I think Stacy is right. We need something that will draw attention to the magazine and attract younger readers."

"So you're not pissed off that I left you after the class?"

"A little disappointed. Frustrated even." She shrugged. "But we both have jobs to do, and it would be foolish and…and unfair for me to resent you shooting all day."

He studied her, trying to determine if she meant the words. If she did, it would be a first for him. But then, Glynna was different from any other women he'd been with. He scooted onto the bed and stretched out beside her.

"What are you doing?" she asked.

"I'm trying to figure you out."

"I thought you'd already done that. Didn't you say I was a 'daddy's girl' who 'jumped when my father said hop.'"

He winced. "Maybe I didn't have the whole story."

She looked away, her smile vanished. "Oh, you had it right. Mostly. I am the blue-blood daughter, raised by my no-nonsense father to do exactly what's expected of me. What else is there to know?"

"What about your mother? Where does she fit in?"

"She died when I was nine. It's been just me and my father since then."

He could picture it now—the grieving widower throwing himself into his work, the little girl trying to capture his attention by following in his footsteps. It had taken her, what, fifteen years to figure out that wasn't enough. He stroked her thigh, her skin cool against his hand. "I think you're more than just your father's daughter."

She looked at him, silent, as if waiting for him to elaborate.

"You're a talented writer. Talented enough to do anything you want if you don't hold yourself back. You're a passionate woman, more daring than you think."

A smile flirted with the corners of her mouth at these words. "I've certainly been more daring this weekend, thanks to you."

"No, it's not all my doing. The potential had to be there. I was just lucky enough to go along for the ride."

A fist clenched at his heart at the words. It had been great to meet up with her. No matter what happened after tomorrow when they returned to Houston, he'd never forget this weekend.

"Maybe I'm the lucky one," she said. "When I worked up the nerve to, well, proposition you last night, I half expected you to laugh in my face."

The words stung, though he tried not to show it. Had she really considered him so callous? "How could you think that?"

"I thought you didn't like me."

"And I was sure you didn't like me." He rested his

hand on her stomach, fingers splayed, savoring the soft warmth of her. "I'm flattered you asked me. I'm still not sure why you did." What did a woman like her see in him?

"You're not like other men I know." She rolled over to face him, to look into his eyes. "You say what you mean. You don't play games or try to impress people. And you never seem to have doubts. I wish I could borrow some of your confidence."

"Oh, I have doubts. All the time." He twined a lock of her hair in his fingers. It slid like silk against his skin. "But I've learned not to show them. Or to ignore them and charge forward anyway."

She smiled. "I guess that's what I did last night. I'm glad."

The warmth of her smile made his heart lurch. If he didn't watch it, his mixed-up emotions would get the better of common sense. He grasped a handful of the silky negligee and tried to keep his voice casual. "So what happens next? Has this weekend changed anything for you?"

She looked away. "I…I don't know. I hope so."

He shoved up into a sitting position and leaned over to kiss her. He was gentle, wanting to encourage more than to inflame. She deserved better than the life she had. He wasn't the one to give it to her, but he would do what he could to help her go after it.

She put her hands on his shoulders and pulled away, smiling. "I've got a surprise for you."

"You do?" He grinned, pleased. "What is it?"

"Look in the closet over there."

He slid off the bed and went to the closet in the corner. He opened it and studied the hanging clothes. Nothing looked out of place or unusual. "I don't see—"

Something soft swept over his head and covered his eyes. He felt her knotting the scarf behind his head and put up his hands to stop her. "No, please," she said. "You'll enjoy this. I promise."

He frowned, but let her lead him to the bed. "I'm not into all this bondage stuff, you know."

"How do you know if you've never tried it?" Her tone was teasing.

"Who says I haven't tried it?" He sat down hard as his legs brushed the edge of the bed and braced himself to resist restraints.

"I think it might be fun some time. But not tonight." She pressed him back. "I only want you blindfolded."

"Why?" He settled himself against the pillows, still unsure if he liked this idea or not.

"As a photographer, you rely on your vision—how you see the world. Color and light and how things look are everything to you. I thought it would be…interesting, if you had to rely on your other senses for a change."

He grunted. He was all for experimenting in the bedroom. And there was something to what she said. "All right. I'll go along with you. For now."

She slid her hand across his belly. Her touch was cool, soft. She moved lower, beneath the waistband of his trunks, down his abdomen, the muscles tightening at her touch. Her fingers dragged through his pubic hair, teasing the underside of his cock. The silk of her negligee floated over his stomach, tickling, the vanilla and spice fragrance of her perfume surrounding him.

Her weight shifted as she knelt beside him. Grasping the waistband of the trunks, she yanked them down over his hips. He raised up, helping her, cool air washing over him as she stripped him.

"You do have the most marvelous body." She brushed her hand across his chest. "Have you ever considered posing nude?"

He laughed. "I spend my time behind the camera lens, not in front of it."

"That's what I thought."

"I don't—" The words were cut off as she blew hot breath on his shaft. He could feel her mouth, inches from him, almost but never quite touching him as she moved up and down, exhaling gently. His penis rose and swayed, demanding attention.

She laughed and moved down. He gasped as her tongue caressed his balls. She took him in her mouth, suckling gently, then teased him again with her tongue. He arched against the mattress, craving more.

Her weight shifted and she leaned away from him. He reached out to pull her back, but she laughed and dodged him.

She was back in a moment, her hands on his chest. "Tell me what this smells like," she said. She began to smooth warm oil across his chest.

He drew in a deep breath. "Cinnamon."

"Very good. How does it feel?" She dripped oil onto first one nipple, then the other, and began to work it in with the tips of her fingers.

"I'll give you twenty minutes to stop that."

"Mmmm." In answer she leaned down and licked off

She leaned down and peered into the viewfinder. "I wanted to see what it was like, being on this side of the lens, looking at the world from this perspective."

"And what do you think?"

"It's…interesting." She swivelled the camera on its tripod. "You can control how things look to a certain extent, by changing the angle or adjusting the lighting." She raised her head and looked at him. "Writers do that, too. We call it slanting the story. Telling it from a particular perspective."

"I thought journalists were supposed to be objective."

"At least as objective as photographers." She left the camera and walked toward him. His gaze focused on her swaying hips.

"We all see things from our own point of view, colored by our experiences, our beliefs and our backgrounds." She knelt on the bed beside him. "But I think…we can all learn to look at things differently too. Maybe things we once thought were important aren't as vital anymore." She put her arms around him and drew him close. "Or we only thought there was one way to do something before, and now we see other ways."

Or a woman he thought was cold and brittle as ice turned out to be soft and warm and sweet as melted chocolate. He kissed her, pulling her down onto the bed as he did so. She wrapped one leg over his hip and plunged her tongue into his mouth, as if she sought to devour him.

The pent-up desire that had been building all day surged through him, so that his hands shook as he stroked her thighs. He pressed her back against the sheets and slid the length of her body, drawn to the sweet wet heat of her sex. He parted her lips and breathed in the musk of her arousal. She arched to him, moaning her pleasure as he teased her with his tongue. She was a wild woman, writhing beneath him, beautiful in her unrestrained desire. He could feel the tension growing as he slipped his hands beneath her bottom, drawing her nearer. He licked and teased, his own need building to the edge of pain.

Her cry of release rocked through him. She was still pulsing beneath him when he rose and took a condom from the bedside table. He quickly tore open the packet, sheathed himself and plunged into her. He thrust hard and fast, her muscles clenching around him, her body arching up to meet his. She grasped his shoulders and looked at him, eyes wide. "I…I think I'm going to come again," she panted.

"Go for it, baby." He reached down to help her along, fighting to hold himself back.

Her eyes glazed over and she gasped her second climax. He let himself go then, following her over the edge, deaf and blind to everything but the white fire that burned through him.

GLYNNA LAY cradled against Jake, waiting for her heart to stop racing and her breathing to slow. How was it that this man could stir her so? Was it their exotic setting, or the strange bargain they had made to only have this one weekend that made every sensation so much more intense? Or was there something more going on here?

She didn't dare explore that idea more closely. Tomorrow she and Jake were leaving here, going back to their everyday lives, where the two of them were no more than co-workers.

He stirred and slipped out of her arms. "Where are you going?" She raised her head to watch him cross the room.

He stopped beside the camera, and fiddled with some dials. "I want to photograph you."

She sat up more, gathering the sheet around her. "No." She could still remember how he had looked through the viewfinder—so beautiful. So…distant.

He rested one hand on the camera and looked at her, his gaze searching, delving. "I photograph people all day. None of them mean anything to me beyond art. Even the women in my gallery showing are just…objects. You're…different. I want to see if I can capture that on film."

The tears that stung her eyes surprised her. Was he saying she *did* mean something to him? Something neither one of them could afford to name? She looked away. "I don't know if I can do it. Expose myself that way."

"I'll pose you so your face is covered. Your eyes, anyway. No one will know it's you. Except you."

Jake would know. Would he look at the photo and think of her? Would the thoughts be good ones? She nodded. "All right. Tell me what to do."

He walked back over to the bed and pulled the sheets away from her. "Lie back against the pillows. That's it." He arranged her legs, one raised with bent knee, the other stretched flat, slightly out to one side. He removed the shade from the bedside lamp and pushed it back until it fell like a spotlight on her. She put one hand up to shield her eyes from the glare.

"No, like this." he took both wrists and lifted her arms over her head, "Now turn your face into your elbow, like that." He stepped back. "That's it. You just made love and drifted to sleep for a brief moment. When you woke, your lover was gone. You're stretching, trying to wake up before you go in search of him."

Why did he say "your lover" and not "me"? she wondered. Was he already distancing himself from her?

He walked back to the camera and bent to look through the viewfinder. She wished she could see what he was seeing now. Did the bright light illuminate every flaw? Was the cellulite on her thighs noticeable? Did her breasts sag? Did she look fat? She wasn't some model— just an ordinary woman with a far from perfect figure. She was crazy to do this. "Jake, I—" She started to sit up.

"No. Lie still. You're beautiful." The shutter clicked, the auto-winder whirred. Once, twice, half a dozen times.

"Jake, please. This feels so strange."

"Why? I've seen you naked before."

"But you've never…stared at me like this. From across the room." She shifted her hips, trying to get more comfortable. But the discomfort she felt was inside her, not in her surroundings. "I feel like…like I'm on display."

"And I like what I see. Can you tell?" He glanced down at his growing erection. He looked at her again. "I've heard modeling can be very erotic. What do you think?"

"I think I'm very lonely on this bed all by myself."

"Do you feel that way at home sometimes?"

All the time. She frowned at him. Where was this question leading? "Everyone does, some time or another. Don't you?"

"Sure." He looked through the viewfinder again. "But I'm talking about you. What do you do when you're lonely?"

"What do you mean?"

"Do you ever take matters into your own hands, so to speak?"

"Sometimes." She squirmed. "But it's not the same." Masturbation was okay for physical release, but the emotional connection she craved was missing. She rolled over onto her side to face him. "Put away the camera and come here."

He raised his head to look at her without the camera between them. "No. I think I want to watch you this time."

"So you can take pictures?" She flushed. "No."

He shut off the camera and stepped away. "No pictures. I promise."

She shook her head. "No."

He grinned. "What can I say? Every photographer is a voyeur at heart. I thought it would be fun to watch."

"If I wanted to satisfy myself, I wouldn't have asked you." She rolled over onto her other side, her back away from him, not wanting him to see how upset she really was. Some other time "performing" for him might be fun. But now they only had a few more hours to be together. She wanted to spend that time as close as two people could be. Not separated by anything.

She didn't hear him cross the room to her, but his

hand on her shoulder was warm, reassuring. "I didn't mean to upset you."

She rolled over onto her back again. "I'm only upset because we don't have much more time."

He nodded. "Tomorrow we go back to the real world. Where the two of us are barely civil to each other."

"It won't be like that anymore." She took his hand in hers. "I'll always think of you as a friend now. But I don't see how we could keep this up when we're back to our regular lives."

He nodded. "I agree. We're headed in two different directions." He leaned over and kissed the side of her mouth while his hand caressed her breast. "It's been a pretty spectacular weekend, though."

"No regrets?"

"No regrets." The words were half-swallowed in a kiss. She closed her eyes and surrendered to his exploring mouth, his stroking hands. Later, she knew there would be tears. Now all she could do was live in the moment, and pray that tomorrow evening when she stepped onto the pier in Galveston, the memory of all they'd done this weekend would somehow change her. That in these moments of daring and desire, she'd discover a hidden reserve of courage she could take into the world to help her find her dreams.

8

"GLYNNA McCORMICK, I want you in my office this minute!"

Glynna winced at the sound of her father's voice on the intercom. Stacy had warned her that today was the day galleys of the upcoming issue of *Texas Style* would land on her father's desk. She'd known he wouldn't be happy. The trick was to find a way to convince him to let the issue go to press. If she couldn't, she could very well be looking for another job.

She paused outside Gordon's office to straighten her jacket and smooth her hair. Then, taking a deep breath, she pushed open the door.

Stacy was there, sitting ramrod straight in a chair in front of Gordon's desk. Glynna's father was on the other side of the desk, hunched over the galley sheets spread before him, a deep vee etched on his brow. At Glynna's entrance, he looked up and the frown deepened. "Where's that photographer?" he barked.

"I...I don't know." She had seen little of Jake in the three weeks since they'd returned from La Paloma. By tacit agreement, they'd avoided one another, though he'd occupied her thoughts often enough. With as much confidence as she could muster, she walked across the room and sat next to Stacy.

The editor gave her a concerned look. Glynna cleared her throat. "I think the cover story for this issue turned out exceptionally well," she said.

"You do, do you?" Gordon picked up the front page of the article on La Paloma. "What's Your Fantasy?" he read the title of the piece. "Do you really think this sort of *pandering* is what the readers of *Texas Style* expect?"

"It's not at all what they expect. That's the whole point." Stacy leaned forward and tapped the cover photo for the issue. "You said you wanted me to update the magazine. This is what young, up-to-date readers want. And those are the kinds of readers advertisers want to attract."

"Readers want garbage like this?"

Glynna winced at the words. They ought not to hurt by now, but they did.

"Have you read the article? Or did you make your judgment based on the photos?"

Her breath caught and she turned as Jake strode into the room. He was dressed in motorcycle leathers, the fringes of his jacket stirring in the draft from the air-conditioning. He didn't look at her, but walked to the desk and picked up the cover photo. "You're wrong about the shots. These are some of my best work. As for the article…" He turned to Glynna, and the heat in his eyes made her sit back in her chair. He looked at Gordon. "Have you read it? Glynna did a damn fine job on it. Or would it kill you to admit that?"

"Jake, sit down." Stacy sent him a warning look.

"No, I think I'll stand." He met Gordon glare for

glare. "It's a quality piece of work," he said. "Good journalism with a pop-culture edge, not sleaze. I think the readers are smart enough to know the difference."

"Oh, they are, are they? And what do you know about my readers?" Gordon's withering look was wasted on Jake, who continued to stare him down. The publisher turned to Glynna. "What do you have to say for yourself?"

Aware of Jake watching her, she fought the urge to shrink back in her chair. She straightened her spine and held her chin up. "I'm proud of the article," she said. "It's different from the investigative reporting I've done in the past, but it's solid work."

She forced herself to look her father in the eye. Did she imagine his look of censure faded? *"Hmmph,"* he grunted. "I did teach you never to do anything halfway." He looked down at the article again. "What happens if we run this? We'll have subscribers canceling in droves."

"Maybe so," Stacy said. "But this is the kind of piece that will get readers talking. People will be grabbing the issue off the newsstands to see what all the fuss is about. When they see it, new readers will subscribe."

Gordon turned his back to them. Glynna studied his still-broad shoulders and thinning hair. He had always reminded her of a bull, stocky and stubborn. Not the kind of man you could cuddle up to. Even when she was small, he'd kept a certain distance between them. Why couldn't she find a way to bridge that gap?

She became aware of someone watching her and turned to find Jake's gaze fixed on her. His lips were pressed together in a frown, but he gave her a slight nod, a gesture of encouragement. She fought back a smile as her heart beat faster. She'd missed him so much. Her condo had seemed twice as empty upon her return from La Paloma, and her nights had been restless, remembering the time she'd spent in his arms.

"It's too late to pull the story now." Gordon turned to face them again. "We'll go with it, but from now on, *I'll* approve the cover stories."

Glynna glanced at Stacy. The editor's face went white, then red. She stood. "You hired me as editor. You have to let me do my job."

"You do your job. But this is my magazine. My name has been on it for almost thirty years, and my wife's family's name was on it before that. Until you prove to me that this is what my readers really want, I have the final say."

Stacy straightened, the picture of icy composure. "Of course. And what would you like for the next issue's cover story?"

Gordon glanced at Jake, then at Glynna. She flinched at the calculating look in his eye. "I think we should have our top reporter and our award-winning photographer team up again. Do a story on something that's the essence of the city."

Glynna relaxed a little. Houston had plenty of interesting possibilities for a story on the "essence of the city." The arts community, historic downtown, oil and cattle...

"I want a story on the ship channel."

Jake's laugh was a harsh bark. "You're kidding me."

Glynna stared at her father. The Houston Ship Channel was a corridor of petrochemical plants, industrial tankers and barges. "You think readers want a story on the ship channel?" Jake shook his head. "Do you want to bore them to death?"

"You're the ones who are supposed to be brilliant." Gordon sat smugly behind his desk. "You should be able to make any subject interesting, right?"

"That's ridiculous," Stacy said. "We can't have a cover story on the ship channel. There's nothing sexy or interesting about it."

"We *will* have a cover story on the ship channel." Gordon's grim look left no room for argument. "And I expect these two to show off that expensive talent I'm paying for and make it interesting."

"But Father—" Glynna rose to protest.

"Come on, Glynna. I've had enough of this." Before she could say anything else, Jake took her arm and pulled her from the room. He didn't say another word or stop walking until they reached her office. Inside, he released his hold on her and shut the door behind them.

"Of all the horrible, dirty tricks!" She began to pace, anger making a hard knot in her chest. "What is he trying to prove? Does he want the magazine to fail?"

"No, he just wants us to fail. Or rather, he wants to put us in our place." Jake walked over to her desk and picked up a stapler, then put it down. "But we won't."

"Oh, sure. Easy for you to say. You can probably make photos of tankers and oil refineries look artistic. But what am I going to write about that readers will pay attention to?" She crossed her arms, wishing he would hug her instead. When he'd stood up for her in her father's office, the flimsy barricades she'd erected around her feelings for him had come tumbling down. Working with him again wasn't going to do anything to help her put them up again.

"You'll find a way to pull it off." His hand on her shoulder was heavy and warm. It took everything in her not to lean into him. "You're a good writer. Some angle will come to you."

She hung her head. "Maybe. I…I wonder if it's even worth trying." She looked at him. "He's never going to see me any differently. I always come up short in his view."

He squeezed her shoulder, then took his hand away. "That's his problem. Don't make it yours." He moved to the door. "I have to go now. When can you meet me to get to work on this?"

She glanced at her desk. As usual, the in-box was piled high. But all that work would wait. She craved any excuse to get out of the office, especially if it meant being with Jake. Being with him made her feel stronger. "Tomorrow? The sooner the better."

"I'll pick you up here tomorrow morning at eight. And don't worry. We'll pull this off."

When he was gone, she slumped against the desk. Jake had faith in her. If only she could find a way to borrow some of that faith for herself.

JAKE RACED ALONG Loop 610, wind rushing against his helmet, the roar of the engine in his ears. One look at Glynna's face in Gordon's office and he'd come as close as he ever had to punching the man. Couldn't he see how much his words hurt her? Or didn't his daughter matter to him?

He slowed to take a sharp curve, hands clenched around the grips. Glynna McCormick was gorgeous, sexy, sweet and she had more talent in her little finger than most journalists had in their whole bodies. But her father had made sure she never saw any of that. If only Jake could find a way to let her in on the secret. He'd like to do that one thing before he took off for New York. He felt he owed her that somehow.

Maybe helping Glynna now would allow him to put aside all the memories of the magic they'd made in La Paloma. He'd developed the photos he'd shot of her. Watching them emerge from the developer bath had been like taking a punch in the gut. He'd been knocked back by desire and a stomach-clenching regret that what they'd shared on the island could never be recreated out here in the "real" world.

He'd stared a long time at the drying photos, his eyes caressing every curve the way his hands had done in the moments before and after the pictures were taken. As a man who'd never suffered a shortage of women in his life, he couldn't explain why that weekend with Glynna had been so different. In those few short days she'd touched him in a way no other woman had.

He accelerated to pass a slow truck and zoomed down a straightaway, as if trying to outrun his own feelings. Life was full of sacrifices and trade-offs, he told himself. If he wanted to go to New York and make a name for himself, he couldn't have Glynna. She needed to stay here and go after her own dreams. He couldn't do much to help her, but he *could* see to it that they made a smash of this story. He wanted to hear her father say she'd done a good job, at least once before he went away.

NICK CASTILLO paused outside Stacy's office to straighten his tie and smooth his hair. Time to turn on the charm. Stacy was a good editor, but like most of them, she didn't give enough credit to the art side. It was up to him to make her see things from his point of view.

Hand poised to knock, he leaned into the open doorway. His smile of greeting faded when he saw Stacy slumped behind her desk, head in her hands. Uh-oh. Maybe now wasn't a good time. He started to back out, but the buttons on the sleeve of his jacket hit the door frame. She jerked her head up, then immediately straightened and assumed a stern expression. "What is it, Nick?"

He stepped into her office and looked around. As usual, everything was in perfect order. Tasteful art on the walls, bound back issues of *Texas Style* arranged in the bookshelf, next to a small lighted display of industry awards. Not a single personal photograph, book or knickknack in the place. Come to think of it, he knew precious little about the shapely editor's personal life. Did she have a boyfriend? An ex?

"Say what you have to say. I'm very busy."

He sat in the chair across from her and looked pointedly at the empty desktop. "I can see that." He was always suspicious of people who kept their desks so orderly. What were they really hiding with their neatness?

She shoved her hair back off her forehead and gave him an annoyed look. All her lipstick had been chewed off. Definitely unlike the meticulous Ms. Southern. "What's going on?" he asked. "You look upset."

She looked away from him, out the window. "I'm sure it will be all over the office this afternoon. Gordon McCormick just raked me over the coals."

The publisher was known for his temper; most of the time the staff laughed off his fits of pique, but this had apparently been something more. Nick settled his elbows on his knees and leaned toward her. "What about?"

"What else? He's furious about this issue's cover story."

"Ahhh." Nick nodded. "The sex resort."

"It's not a sex resort," she snapped. "It's a sensuous, romantic getaway."

"But definitely not the magazine's usual style."

"Which was the whole point." She tucked her hair behind one ear. "I told him I was going to take us away from the staid image that had us losing ground with subscribers and advertisers. When he hired me, he said that was exactly what he wanted."

"Sometimes people only think they want something, until they get it." Why hadn't he noticed before how soft and shiny her hair was? A kind of silvery gold color, only a few shades darker than her peaches-and-cream skin.

"And *some* people are smart enough to see when they get something that it's even better than they anticipated."

"Hey, I'm on your side here." He picked up the cover mock-up for the upcoming issue. Jake's photo of a couple floating in the ocean while the sun set behind them was a stunner, the kind of thing that would stop traffic at the newsstand. "When people see this, we'll be the talk of the town," he said.

She made a face. "And the next issue they'll be treated to a spectacular story about the ship channel."

He laughed, thinking she was joking, but one look at her stormy eyes told him this was no jest. "You're kidding."

She shook her head. "Gordon told Glynna and Jake to do a piece on the ship channel. How is that going to sell magazines? Not to mention that *I'm* the editor. I'm supposed to be assigning stories. Why else did he hire me?"

He laid aside the galleys. "So what are you going to do about it?"

She sat back in her chair and sighed. "Maybe I should start looking for another job."

"Or maybe you should do this one so well he can't afford to let you go."

She shook her head. "What's the point?"

Seeing her like this disturbed him. She was usually such a take-charge type. Intimidating even. Not his type, but there was something…energizing…about working with a woman who was so sure of what she wanted. "I thought you had more guts than that," he said.

He almost smiled at the anger that flashed in her eyes. She sat up straighter, legs crossed at the knee to reveal several inches of pale thigh. She had great legs. Another nice thing about working with her. "Don't you have work to do? Or is there some point to your visit?"

She had her claws out now. This was the Stacy he knew. He sat back, relaxing in the chair as if he intended to stay all day, knowing the posture would annoy her. "I think it's time we did a photo-essay. Something edgy and artistic. Images that will get readers talking."

She looked skeptical. "How many pages are we talking about?"

"At least eight. I want something with meat on it. Maybe even a cover story—told only in photographs."

She shook her head. "I don't have that much space to work with. And whoever heard of a cover story with no copy?"

He leaned forward again. "Exactly. You want cutting edge. That's cutting edge."

She looked unconvinced. "People won't buy a magazine just to look at pictures."

"Says who? Haven't you heard a picture is worth a thousand words?"

"Not the right thousand words."

"People react to the visual. Photos immediately affect their emotions. Words take more work to process."

"Are you saying our readers are lazy?"

"Of course they are. People are." He gave her a heated look. "Think about it. Would you rather see a naked man, or have someone describe him to you?"

"It depends on the man." Her gaze swept over him, bold and unflinching. "Would you rather see a woman who's aroused or have her tell you how you make her feel?"

Her words, and her look, kindled an immediate reaction in his groin. He swallowed. "How about 'all of the above'?"

Her eyes smiled, though her lips remained impassive. "I suppose you have someone in mind to do the photos?"

"Of course. Jake Dawson."

She rolled her eyes. "Gordon will love that. More of his least favorite photographer."

"But he's the readers' favorite."

"Do you have a particular subject in mind?"

"I'll leave that up to Jake. Or to you."

She drummed her fingers on the desk. She had long nails, meticulously done in a French manicure. He liked women who did that. There was something erotic about the sight of long nails resting against his skin.

"Maybe a piece on public art," she mused, interrupting his daydreaming. "Or city parks?"

"I'm sure you can think of something. Use your imagination."

Her eyes met his. "I have a very good imagination."

"Do you?" *And would you like to try it out on me?*

She stood up and walked to the window, giving him a good look at those long legs and shapely backside. So what if he preferred someone younger? Someone softer? There was nothing wrong with enjoying the view.

She turned suddenly, and her half smile told him she knew exactly where his eyes had been focused. "If I do this for you, what are you going to do for me?"

He let his gaze drop to her legs again. "What did you have in mind?" He could think of a few suggestions, most of which involved them both naked.

She licked her lips, a blatant, sensuous gesture that put his libido on red alert. "I'll have to think about it and get back to you."

He shoved up out of the chair, buttoning his jacket over the erection he was sure was evident. "You do that," he said. "I can't wait." He left the office before she could say more. His policy was to make a woman want him, not the other way around. Stacy Southern was the first women he'd met in a long time who might be better than he at playing the game.

AS GLYNNA WAITED for Jake in her office the next morning, she couldn't stop pacing. Her insides felt raw from wrestling all night with her worries about this story. Could she really make such a dull subject entertaining?

Worse, she was furious with her father for giving her this test and for the way he'd discounted her all these years. She'd lain awake half the night writing speeches in her head she should make to him. But this morning, when she'd passed him in the office hallway and he had nodded formally and said "Good morning, Glynna," the way he always did—as if she were any other drone working in the office instead of his only daughter—all the courage she'd mustered had faded away. What did it matter anyway? She couldn't expect to change his feelings with a few heartfelt words.

And then there was the whole problem of how to handle Jake. How was she supposed to spend time alone with him working on this story and keep to their bargain of "just friends"? What she felt for him was so much more complicated than that. How could it not be awkward between them, when she was still so attracted to him? When the memory of all they'd shared on the island was so fresh in her mind?

Just then the man himself appeared at her door. He was dressed in jeans and a khaki photographer's vest over a denim shirt with the sleeves rolled up to the elbows, his hair tousled, his face slightly flushed beneath his tan from his morning ride over on his bike. "Are you ready to go?"

"I guess so." She grabbed up her leather messenger bag and slung it over one shoulder. For schlepping around the ship channel, she'd worn jeans, low-heeled boots and an embroidered gauze shirt and tied her hair back with a silk scarf.

She followed Jake down the hall to the elevator. They didn't speak while they waited for the doors to open, but she was aware of his eyes on her. She folded her arms across her chest, self-conscious. When he looked at her, did he remember what she looked like without her clothes? She wanted to ask him about the photos he'd taken of her, but that topic seemed too charged to bring up now.

"What angle have you come up with for the story?" he asked after a minute.

"I don't have one. I'm hoping inspiration will strike as I research."

"I've got an idea for you."

She glanced at him, surprised. "What's that?"

"Your old man wants the ship channel. Stacy wants sexy and hip. Why not give them all three?"

She made a face. "How do we do that?"

He grinned. "We give them the sexy side of the ship channel."

She laughed. "I didn't know there was one."

"I think there is. And I'm about to show it to you."

The elevator arrived and they stepped on, standing apart and facing forward, like strangers who worked in the same building. All this talk of sexy stories led her mind right back to their weekend at La Paloma. Her gaze was drawn to his reflection in the mirrored doors; he was watching her. A small sigh escaped her. "This is never going to work," she said.

"What do you mean?" He turned toward her.

The elevator doors opened in the parking garage and she stepped out. He was right behind her, his hand on her arm. "What won't work?"

"Us. Together." She clenched her fists and stared at the ground, fighting to appear cool when inside she was burning up with wanting him. "I thought I could keep things casual between us, but…my body doesn't agree. It still remembers how you made me feel." The last words came out as a whisper. Her face was hot. He probably saw her as some sex-starved spinster who'd gotten in over her head. Maybe there was some truth in that assessment, but she couldn't change what she felt.

"Yeah."

The one word, sounding as if it had been dragged from somewhere deep inside him, startled her. She raised her eyes to meet his and recognized a pain close to what she was feeling.

He quickly masked the emotion with forced mirth. "Yeah, hormones are hell, aren't they?" He shoved his hands in his pockets and looked out over the garage. "We had a great time at La Paloma, but we both know it wouldn't work, us being together. As soon as I can, I'm headed to New York, and you've got a whole different life here in Houston."

Was this his way of saying he wasn't interested? She

touched his arm and felt the muscles bunch beneath her fingers, heard the catch of his breath. A flutter of triumph stirred in her chest. Jake still wanted her all right. And she wanted him. Who cared if he didn't intend to stay in town? Why not enjoy each other while they could?

He shrugged out of her grasp and started across the parking lot. "Come on. We'd better get going."

She followed, the sound of her heels striking the concrete echoing in the cavernous garage. She'd have to think about this a while longer, look for a way to persuade him that a temporary liaison would be good for them both, though part of her mind warned her she was playing with live ammo to even suggest such a thing.

He stopped beside a hulking black-and-chrome motorcycle and unstrapped two helmets. "Put this on," he ordered, handing her a white one.

She looked at it, stunned. "I thought we'd go in my car."

"My bike's easier to get around in traffic, easier to park." He fastened his own helmet and swung his leg over the bike. "Come on. It'll be fun."

She took a step back. Hurtling through traffic straddling a loud, racing engine wasn't her idea of a good time. "I'll drive then, and meet you wherever we're going."

He reached out and grabbed her hand and pulled her toward him. "Come on. Where's the woman I saw at La Paloma who was willing to take a few risks?"

He certainly knew how to push her buttons, she thought, as she fastened her chin strap and climbed on the bike behind him. She put her feet on the foot rests, then looked for some hold for her hands.

"Put your arms around me," he said.

She opened her mouth to argue, but he jumped down on the starter and the engine rumbled to life. With a squeal, she threw her arms around him and pressed her face against his back. The masculine aromas of leather and oil were strangely comforting. Jake seemed solid and real in a world that was hurtling by her. If she could only keep her grip on him until she figured out what direction she was supposed to go with her life.

9

JAKE LIKED THE FEEL of Glynna riding behind him. At first, she had clung to him as if her life depended on it, her head pressed hard against his back, her arms squeezing him tightly. But gradually she had relaxed, though she still leaned close to him. He was aware of the curve of her breasts on his back, her thighs pressed tight along his.

She'd surprised him there in the elevator, when she'd admitted to wanting him. In the weeks they'd been apart, he'd convinced himself that their wild weekend had meant nothing to her. How else to explain her cool reserve at the office? Whenever he was near, she never looked at him, while he could scarcely take his eyes off of her. It grated that a woman could take hold of him this way, but he'd resigned himself to learning to deal with it.

Then their gazes had locked in the elevator and he'd seen that her feelings for him were anything but cold. It would have been so easy to take her in his arms right there and satisfy his lust for her.

But where would that get him? Thinking about her these past few weeks had been enough of a distraction from his work. Getting involved with her again would take time and energy he didn't have. Better to spend that effort putting together a portfolio to wow New York galleries and agents. Once he left town, it wouldn't be so hard to get Glynna out of his mind.

He hoped.

He slowed the bike to turn onto Clinton Drive. As they rolled through the gates to Port Eight, Glynna pressed forward and spoke in his ear. "Where are we going?"

"We're going go take a tour of the channel."

He parked the bike and helped Glynna off. "I don't know if I'm steady enough to walk," she said, clutching his arm. "I haven't been that terrified in a long time."

"You did great. And we arrived in one piece, didn't we?" Not that he hadn't suffered a few strained nerves himself, what with the way she'd plastered herself against him. He could tell right now he was going to need a cold shower when he got home.

She finger-combed her hair and turned to look at the white cabin cruiser with its shaded observation deck and the name *Sam Houston* on the bow. "Free tours." She read the sign at the end of the gangway, then looked at him. "This is the sexy side of the ship channel?"

"Part one." He put a hand to her back and nudged her toward the end of the dock. "You'll see."

She resisted. "Are you forgetting I get seasick? There won't be anything sexy about that."

"I didn't forget." He dug in the pocket of his vest and pulled out a cardboard packet of pills. "Take these. They'll help."

She looked doubtful, but pulled a bottle of water from her bag and swallowed the pills. Then they joined a small group of people waiting to board the *Sam Houston*—two older couples, a mother with four children in tow and an older man. After a few minutes, a man in a crisp white uniform came to welcome them to the ship.

When they boarded, Jake led her up two flights of narrow stairs to the very top of the craft. "I want to see everything," he said.

The diesel engines of the boat rumbled beneath them and the smell of oil, fish and salt was anything but erotic. Jake checked his lenses and filters and hoped this would work out. If it didn't, they'd have to go to plan B, and he had no idea what that was.

A recording came on the loudspeaker, welcoming them to the *Sam Houston* inspection ship and outlining the safety information. Then the boat began to slowly back out of the dock.

When they were under way, Glynna stood and walked to the railing on the port side. Jake followed her. The voice on the loudspeaker informed them that the Port of Houston was ranked first in the United States in foreign waterborne commerce, second in total tonnage and was eighth overall in the world.

He scanned the crowded port, then pointed. "Okay, there's something to mention in the article. Those yachts over there."

He indicted a trio of gleaming white yachts that rose out of the water like ocean-going castles. "Some of the wealthiest people come here from all over the world to do business." He aimed his camera and clicked off half a dozen shots.

"Of course. And we all know money is sexy," she said.

"Not having any sure isn't an aphrodisiac."

The rusting gray sides of a tanker ship jutted up in front of them like a fortress wall. He leaned back to check the colors snapping in the breeze on the bow. "Liberia," he said. "There are ships here from all over the world—Greece, Spain, Japan, Russia. You can walk along the docks and hear ten different languages in as many minutes."

She leaned back against the railing, hair whipping behind her. "All right, you've convinced me. Maybe the ship channel isn't all dirty water and diesel fumes."

He gripped the camera more tightly, fighting the urge to pull her into his arms and kiss her until they were both dizzy and breathless. He turned away and focused the camera on a departing freighter. "That's the beauty of this story. We'll show people what they aren't expecting."

"You're right. It's a good idea." They passed a refinery, with its tangle of pipes, stacks and cooling towers jutting up like trees in a dense forest. The guide on the loudspeaker informed them that 175,000 barrels of oil a day were processed in the port area.

Jake snapped pictures. "These shots are great."

"It's sort of an urban jungle," she said. "Exotic in its own way, though we take it for granted."

"Exactly." He lowered the camera and found she had moved away from the railing. "Where are you going?" he asked.

"Downstairs. I want to see what the rest of the ship is like."

GLYNNA HAD little interest in the ship's mahogany trimmed cabin or brass-lined portholes, but she'd needed to get away from Jake for a while. His insistence on them keeping things strictly business grated. Why was he being so damn sensible? He was supposed to be the wild bad boy. Who would have thought he'd let principles and common sense get in the way of pleasure?

They passed tugboats, refueling barges and acres of oil storage tanks. She watched out a porthole and exchanged pleasantries with the mother and children and one of the older couples. She arranged to go forward and interview the captain, who regaled her with tales of his twenty years piloting ships in the area. Forty-five minutes into the tour, a crew member passed out complimentary soft drinks and announced they would be heading back to the docks.

They were pulling into the slip again when Jake found her. "Ready for our next look at sex and the ship channel?"

"All right." She didn't hesitate to climb on the bike this time. Her initial fear of the machine had faded, replaced by a grudging interest. She still thought motorcycles were dangerous, but she saw the appeal of traveling fast with no barriers around you. Snuggled against Jake, her breasts resting on the hard plane of his back, she could almost forget the risk.

She halfway expected Jake to point out the erotic possibilities of tank farms or petrochemical plants. Instead, she found herself getting off the bike in front of a row of windowless structures painted garish colors.

Nude Dancers, Lunch Buffet, Cocktails proclaimed the marquee above the buildings.

Color washed over her face and she turned to glare at him. "This is a strip joint."

"The politically correct term is 'gentlemen's club.'" He took her hand. "Come on. Let's take a look."

She hung back. "I can't go in there."

"Sure you can. Women do it all the time. Usually with their boyfriends or husbands, but I've seen them in these places alone, too."

Her eyes narrowed. "Why am I not surprised to learn that you're familiar with dives like this?"

"Come on, it's not what you think."

"Oh, so it's not a bunch of silicon-enhanced dancers taking off their clothes for a bunch of ogling men?"

"Last time I checked, it wasn't a crime to look. And let's face it. Men like to watch."

Remembered desire sizzled through her at his words. He'd told her he liked to watch, that last time they were together. "All right. I'll go in there. But if I don't like it, I'm leaving right away."

"Fair enough. Just look around and get some fodder for your story. Consider it a sacrifice for the sake of journalism."

As if she hadn't already given up too much for her career—she'd pretty much sacrificed her life to get to where she was. And now she was prowling around the dockside strip clubs?

JAKE PAID a tired-looking old woman at the door and tugged Glynna inside. She clung to his arm, fingers digging into his sleeve, her steps dragging. "Don't be nervous," he said, slipping his arm around her and pulling her close. He told himself he only wanted to comfort her, but the feel of her plastered against him on the bike had teased him to an almost painful state of arousal. It was all he could do not to take her into some dark corner and put an end to his self-imposed "just friends" edict. Instead, he settled for holding her in this supposedly innocent way.

Beyond the small foyer, the club was very dark. It took a moment for his eyes to adjust to the gloom. There wasn't that much to see: A gray curtain of smoke hovered over a few men seated at a bar next to a runway. A bored-looking blonde with a passing resemblance to Britney Spears was gyrating around a pole with remarkable agility while an Aerosmith song played in the background.

Glynna glanced at the woman, then quickly looked away. Though he couldn't be sure in the dimness, Jake was sure she was blushing. He squeezed her hand and led her to a table near the stage. "Do we have to sit so close?" she asked.

"Yes." He pulled out a chair and after a moment she sat. He pulled his own seat close to hers, so that their knees were touching beneath the table.

A waitress in hot pants and a shiny green halter top hurried over to them. Glynna ordered a Diet Coke and Jake asked for orange juice. "You want anything in that?" the waitress asked.

"No thanks. Just juice."

Glynna leaned over to whisper into his ear, her breath

stirring his hair, sending shivers down his spine. "That's going to make an interesting item on your expense report."

"I'll mark it down as lunch with you."

She sucked in her breath. "You wouldn't dare tell anyone we came here."

"Why not? It's research, isn't it? If you're going to write about the sexy side of the ship channel, you have to mention the strip joints. They do a booming business among the seamen and stevedores, not to mention local businessmen."

"My father will have a stroke if he thinks I came to a place like this."

"It might do him good to acknowledge you have a life outside of work. Including a sex life."

She clamped her mouth shut and looked away. He found himself wondering who would be her next partner. Would another man be smart enough to see past her cool exterior to the fiery woman within? Or would she seek someone out, the way she'd done with him? What if she chose the wrong man, someone who would take advantage of her innocence?

Frowning, he looked away, to the woman on stage. The blonde had stripped down to a G-string and pasties now, her perfect firm breasts bouncing slightly with every dip and sway. The smile on her lips didn't extend to her heavily mascaraed eyes. Jake had always considered himself a man who appreciated the feminine form in all its variations, especially when the form was practically naked. But the woman on stage failed to move him. The memory of Glynna's shapely curves was too fresh in his mind. And the woman herself beside him was definitely a distraction.

He turned to Glynna. She was watching the blonde, her expression equal parts revulsion and fascination. "What do you think?" he asked.

She glanced at him. "I don't see how she can do it."

"It's not exactly Hollywood choreography." He looked back at the stage as the blonde twirled around the pole. "She's pretty good, though. Some of them don't dance that well."

Glynna made a face. "I have a feeling the clients don't come here for the dancing."

Their drinks arrived. The tab was ten dollars. Another line on the expense report. He'd been teasing her when he'd said he'd itemize it as lunch with her. Still, he was tempted. Wasn't it time Gordon McCormick treated his daughter like a flesh-and-blood woman instead of an automaton programmed to do his bidding?

She held her glass to the light. "Do you think this is really clean?" she whispered.

"They serve food, so the health department probably comes around some time."

She pushed her drink aside and looked at him. "So what's the big attraction of places like this?"

"Isn't it obvious? Men like to watch naked women." The blonde was on her knees now before a group of appreciate young men who were slipping ones and fives beneath the elastic of her G-string.

Glynna frowned at the line of men. "You said yourself, they can't do anything with them. So what's the point? Do they just go home and jack off?"

"Sometimes. Or they go home to their wives and girlfriends, ready for action. Or they make a street-corner business deal. You can buy anything you want somewhere on these docks, including sex, drugs and rock and roll."

"How do you know so much about it?" Her voice held a steely edge. Was it the comment about prostitutes that had set her off, or something else?

"I worked as a dockhand summers during high school. Loading cured hides onto container ships destined for overseas leather processing plants." He grimaced, remembering the filthy, backbreaking work. He'd been a boy, doing a man's job and earning a man's pay for it. He sipped the juice. "With my first paycheck, I bought my first really good camera. After I got off work, I'd hang around the docks, taking photos. One of those shots won me a scholarship to Rice University." Rice was one of the most academically challenging schools in the state. It also had a first-rate art department.

Her eyes widened. "I'm impressed."

"You and my grandmother." He looked up at the stage. The woman had finished her dance and was gathering up scattered clothing as she retreated down the runway.

"How old do you think she is?" Glynna asked.

"I don't know. Eighteen? Nineteen?" At one time, he would have appreciated such youth, but there was something to be said for a more mature woman.

"Too young to drink the overpriced liquor they sell here, but old enough to take her clothes off for strangers. Why do they do it?"

"Let's find out." He raised his hand and motioned the girl over. She put on a transparent half shirt and came over to them, frowning. "We're reporters, doing a story on the ship channel area," he said. "Can we talk to you a minute?"

The girl shrugged and sat down at their table. "If I sit here, you have to buy me a drink."

He signaled the waitress. The girl, who told them her name was Kitty, ordered a bottle of champagne. "A glass," he said. "We're not going to be here that long."

When the waitress had left, Glynna turned to the girl. She was pretty, though with her heavy makeup, it was hard to tell her age. "How long have you been dancing here?" she asked.

"About a year." The girl studied her long nails.

"Do you like it?"

Kitty looked bored. "Yeah. It's okay."

Glynna rolled her eyes at Jake. He leaned toward the girl. "Glynna and I were talking just now. She was wondering why a woman would choose to take off her clothes for strangers."

Kitty laughed. "Why not?" She sat up straighter, breasts thrust out. "I got a great body. Why not show it off? And where else can I make this kind of money? And I don't have to break any laws or sleep with anyone to get it."

Glynna twirled her untouched drink. "Isn't it dangerous?" She looked around. "This is a rough neighborhood."

Kitty tapped her nails on the table. "It's not suburbia, but I'm careful. Everybody who works here looks out for each other."

"So the risk is worth it for the money?"

"The money, and…"

"And what?" Glynna leaned forward, clearly fascinated. "What is it about stripping that you like?"

Kitty glanced around them. "In here, women have all the power. I've got a line of men watching, waiting for the next little piece of cloth to drop. I can play to that. Collect the tips, and then walk off. The men are left frustrated and broke."

"Ouch!" Jake said.

Kitty smiled. "Maybe for some women, it's a matter of payback."

The waitress asked if they wanted another drink. Jake pushed his empty glass away. "No thanks. We'd better be going." He slipped a bill to Kitty, who tucked it into her G-string. "Stick around for the next hour and lap dances are half price." She glanced at Glynna. "Some women get off on watching."

"Uh, no thanks." Glynna grabbed her purse and walked past them, out to the parking lot.

Jake met up with her at his bike. "So you don't think you'd get off on watching?"

She whirled to face him, two bright spots of red high on her cheekbones. "Watching you with another woman? Why? Would you get off on watching me with another man?"

The image this conjured in his mind made his jaw tighten, but not from arousal. "No, I don't think I'd want to see that," he admitted.

She glanced at the flashing sign. "There's a difference between sexy and sleazy."

"Sometimes sleazy can be sexy." He strapped on his helmet.

"If you're a man, maybe." She looked back at the glaring neon.

"Maybe sex is only sleazy if it's for sale." He turned to face her. "If Kitty strips for strangers for money, that's sleazy. If a woman does a striptease for her boyfriend, that's sexy."

Her gaze met his, unflinching, probing. She took a step toward him and flattened her hand against his chest, the warmth of her fingers seeping through the fabric to his skin. "If *I* stripped for *you,* would it be sexy?"

He swallowed hard, and his heart raced beneath her palm. How many nights—and days—had he spent dreaming about Glynna naked before him again? He grasped her wrist and pulled her hand away. "If you stripped for me it would be a bad idea," he said.

"It was a pretty good idea on the island."

"Yeah, well, this isn't the island. I thought we agreed." He released her and turned to mount the bike.

She climbed on behind him, and pressed her body against his, deliberately teasing him, he was sure. He'd asked for it, hadn't he? Why had he brought her here? Why had he suggested this stupid topic for the story? As if he needed any more reminders about sex when he was with her.

"I'm not asking you for anything but what you want to give." Her voice was a low purr against his back.

"Right now, that's too much." He revved the engine and the bike roared across the parking lot, back onto Clinton Drive. Glynna was the rare woman who took hold of a man heart and soul. One weekend with her wasn't enough; would one month or one year satisfy him, either? Later in his life, he could commit to a woman that way, but not now. He had other dreams to chase, and Glynna couldn't be a part of those.

THEY DROVE to an observation point overlooking the turning basin. "I want to get some shots here."

While he took photographs, Glynna perched on the bike and made notes. Visiting the strip club had been a disorienting experience. On one hand, she'd been repulsed by the garish display of sex—by the line of panting men and the bored girl gyrating in front of them.

But part of her had been attracted to the scene, as well. What would it be like to have men begging for you that way?

Or maybe not a lot of men. One man.

She glanced at Jake. Engrossed in his work, he leaned over the railing to get a shot of a tanker maneuvering through the basin. She could still remember how his muscular thighs and butt felt beneath her hand. She thought of sneaking up behind him now and goosing him, but if he dropped his expensive camera, he'd probably never forgive her.

She sighed and looked away, at the cars and trucks zipping by on the highway. Heat shimmered off the pavement and she wished she was still resting by the pool at La Paloma. Jake was right: This wasn't a fantasy island where the only thing the two of them had to worry about was each other.

But what was wrong with enjoying what they could, while they could? Yes, they both had jobs and ambitions. And Jake was going away. But she'd spent so many years denying herself things she wanted because she thought it was the right thing to do. She was tired of that now. Why should they keep fighting this feeling that sizzled between them like St. Elmo's fire?

She glanced back at him. He was packing up his camera now. What would he do if she *did* decide to strip for him? Would he turn away from her then? She thought of their last night together, when he'd told her he liked to watch, and smiled. Maybe that was the key to breaking through his self-imposed reserve.

"What are you smiling about?"

She jumped, unaware he'd been watching her. "What?"

He walked over and stowed the camera in his saddlebags. "Just now. You had this really big smile on your face."

"Oh, I had a sudden inspiration." She shifted around to straddle the bike. "You know the feeling, when you get a really great idea."

"Yeah. So what's your idea?"

"I can't talk about it yet." Her smile broadened. "But I promise, you'll find out soon. Very soon."

10

It took Glynna another twenty-four hours to work up the courage to go through with her little plan. Would she come across as too desperate, or would Jake see this as a bold move on her part? It was the kind of thing she wouldn't have done even a few weeks ago. That had to be a good thing, right? Today, she'd seduce the man she wanted. Tomorrow, she'd go after her dream job. Or maybe even stand up to her father.

She buzzed Jake's office Wednesday morning and asked him to stop by her office so she could see the photo proofs for the article. "I'm hoping the pictures you took will give me some more ideas," she said.

"Okay. I can drop them off this afternoon. I'll have all the proofs by then."

"Great. I can't wait."

She spent the rest of the morning trying to set the stage for seduction. She slanted the blinds to soften the light in the room and checked to make sure the lock on the door worked. Then she waited, sitting on her hands to keep from biting her nails. Could she really go through with this?

Jake arrived shortly after one, the sleeves of his

denim shirt rolled to the elbows, motorcycle chaps over his jeans. He filled up her office with his presence, overwhelming the sterile aluminum-and-glass surroundings. He strode past her and dropped his saddlebag onto the sofa across from her desk. "I can't talk long. I've got five rolls of negatives to print to send out tomorrow."

Would he be so eager to leave when he found out what she had in mind? "I won't waste your time," she said. "Sit down and make yourself comfortable."

She motioned to the sofa. While he settled himself there and took several envelopes from his bag, she closed the door and locked it. He looked up from the proof sheets he'd been studying. "What did you do that for?"

"Because I don't want anyone walking by and seeing what we're doing."

He raised one eyebrow and let the proof sheets drop into his lap. "What are we doing?"

"Actually, you're not doing anything." She sat on the edge of her desk. The short skirt of her suit rode up her thighs, revealing the tops of her stockings and the tapes of her garter belt. She spread her legs wider.

His gaze flickered to her crotch, which was almost exactly at eye level now. "That's not a very ladylike way to sit," he said.

"I know. I'm sure most people who know me would be shocked." She spread her legs wider. The draft from the air-conditioning was cool across her naked flesh.

He swallowed. "Do you always go around with no underwear on?"

"Only since I met you. You've done terrible things to corrupt me."

He shifted his gaze to her eyes. "I thought we agreed we shouldn't get involved again."

"Involvement requires two people." She stretched out her leg and rested the toe of her shoe against his shoulder. "Right now, you don't have to do anything but sit back and watch." She pressed him back against the sofa. "You once told me you like to watch, remember?"

Desire sparked in his eyes. He sank back against the cushions and focused his gaze on her crotch once more. "Oh, yeah. I like to watch."

She leaned back and pressed the button on the stereo that sat on the credenza beside her desk. Soft jazz filled the air around them. She hoped it would drown out any noise she might make. The closed door was enough to spark gossip, but with luck no one had seen Jake come in here. She'd planned it that way. She wanted to give him something to think about, not get them both into trouble.

She inched the skirt up higher. Jake sucked in his breath as she bunched the fabric at her waist and revealed her nakedness framed by the lacy garters and sheer stockings. She smiled. She was already wet with anticipation. It had been all she could do to get through the morning waiting for him.

Eyes locked to his, she began to unbutton her blouse. She took her time, letting her fingers graze her skin, taking her cues from Jake. He settled more comfortably on the sofa, long legs stretched out in front of him, his eyes tracking her movements. As the front of the blouse parted, he let out a sigh.

She cupped her breasts with both hands. They felt hot

and heavy, the nipples rigid against the thin satin of her bra. "Do you want to see?" she asked.

He nodded, his answer almost a grunt.

Smiling, she popped open the front catch and pushed aside the silk. She pinched her nipples between thumb and forefinger, a fresh wave of heat and dampness rushing to her groin. Jake's eyes darkened.

"Does it make you hard, watching me?" she asked.

He wet his lips. "What do you think?"

Her gaze dropped to the prominent ridge along his fly. "Show me."

He blinked. "What?"

"Show me how hard you are. Undo your pants."

He hesitated only a second before reaching down to unfasten the button and zipper. He pulled down his briefs, freeing his shaft. "What are you going to do about it?"

"I wanted to see it for…inspiration." Could she really do what she'd planned? Alone, it had been easy to imagine, but here in her office, in the middle of the afternoon, with him watching, it seemed impossibly wanton.

"I'm waiting," he said.

She licked her lips. "Waiting for what?"

"To see where inspiration leads you." He shifted his gaze to her crotch. "If you dare."

That was the bottom line, wasn't it? Was she brave enough to step out of her conventional role, if it meant getting something she really wanted?

She reached down and touched herself. The sharp rush of Jake's breath sent a fresh flood of heat through her. Tentatively, she slid one finger deep inside, her vision losing focus as her thumb dragged across her clit.

Jake leaned forward, eyes fixed on her hand as she slid her finger slowly in and out. "Do you think about us sometimes?" she asked. "Making love there on the island?" She licked the forefinger of her free hand and brought it down to fondle her clit. "I do. I lie awake at night and…and think about how you made me come." Her breath came in gasps, making talking difficult. She blinked, trying to fix her gaze on him, fighting the urge to lean back and close her eyes, to give in to the rush of sensation that beckoned.

He sat back now, his hands gripping the sides of the sofa cushions. The muscles of his thighs tensed, his erection very rigid and dark red, straining toward her. "Do you think about us?" she asked again.

"All the damn time," he growled. "How am I supposed to get any work done?"

"You can see how much you're distracting me," she said. "Can you imagine me doing anything like this before I met you?"

"I imagine all kinds of things about you now." His eyes met hers for a brief moment. "Mostly, I think of you naked."

"Is this close enough?" She brought her hand up again to caress her breasts.

He stood and took a step toward her. "It's close enough."

"No, wait. You're only supposed to watch." She planted her foot against his chest, the high heel scraping against his shirt.

He wrapped his hand around her ankle, then bent and kissed the top of her foot. The touch of his mouth sent fresh desire skittering through her. She gasped, her hand pausing.

"Don't stop," he said, his words muffled as he kissed his way up her calf. "I'm still watching."

She closed her eyes and tried to concentrate again on her own pleasure, but she was distracted by his closeness, by the memory of how good he would feel inside her.

She felt him tugging her hand and opened her eyes as he brought her fingers to his mouth. "Sometimes I wake up, remembering how you taste," he said, his voice gruff. He lowered her hand to her clit once more. "Go on now. I'm still watching." He stroked his hands along her thighs, pushing them farther apart. "I want to watch you come."

She closed her eyes and let her head fall back, her hand moving faster, surer. He continued to stroke her, murmuring encouragement, the sound of his voice, heavy with wanting, driving her over the edge. She arched off the desk, teeth clenched against a scream, her whole body pulsing with release.

Before she had opened her eyes, she heard the sound of a foil packet being ripped open. He put his hands on her hips and slid her forward, to the edge of the desk, then sank into her with a force that stole her breath. With his first withdrawal and thrust she began to climb again.

The coffee mug in which she kept pencils rattled and began a dance across the desk. Paper clips jumped in their holder and documents cascaded from neat piles. She gripped the edge of the desk to keep from sliding off, and he wrapped one arm around her to hold her more securely. At the same time, he bent his head and began to suckle first one breast, then the other.

"Is it as good as you remember?" he whispered. "Or better?"

"The best," she breathed, as she surrendered again to the wonderful, terrifying moment when the two of them were closer than any two souls could ever be. She heard his own guttural cry, and felt his face buried against her neck as he drove against her again and again. Gradually he stilled, and wrapped both arms around her to hold her close. She encircled him with her arms and legs, clinging like a shipwreck victim to a piece of driftwood. No matter what happened next, everything was perfect in this moment. She didn't want to think about the future anymore.

But Jake reminded her anyway. He unwrapped his arms from around her and gently pushed her away. "We'd better get dressed. If someone comes looking for either of us, things could get sticky."

"Things already are sticky." She plucked a tissue from the box on the corner of the desk to wipe herself.

He wrapped the condom in a second tissue and stuck it in his pocket. "What are you doing?" she asked.

"I'm not leaving this in your office for the janitor to find."

She laughed. "Don't have a crash on the way home or there'll be all kinds of questions."

He finished fastening his pants, then turned to watch as she buttoned her blouse and tucked it back into her skirt. "We still have a lot of questions between us, don't we?"

"I'm not trying to make any claim on you, I promise." She turned to face him, hoping she looked more self-confident than she felt. "I only missed being with you." She'd do anything she could to make their relationship last a little longer, even if it meant lying to herself.

He looked away, rubbing the back of his neck. "Yeah. I missed being with you, too." He glanced at her. "You know I'm going to New York as soon as I can swing it."

She nodded. "I know." She blinked hard, commanding herself to stay dry-eyed. If this was going to work, she had to make him think she was in this for the great sex, nothing more. She reached up and smoothed the collar of his shirt. "That doesn't mean we can't enjoy ourselves 'til then, does it?"

He covered her hand with his own and gave it a gentle squeeze. "No, it doesn't." He slipped his other hand around her waist and drew her close. "Can you come over to my place tonight?"

They'd just made love and already he was planning when they could be together again. The idea thrilled her. "I promised my father I'd have dinner with him, but I can try to get away early."

"Good. I want you to see the photos I took of you."

"The ones from La Paloma?" Her stomach clenched. She'd hoped since he'd never mentioned those photos that they hadn't come out.

"They're great," he said, smoothing his hand across her bottom. "You look amazing."

She glanced away. "I don't know if I want to see them."

"Aren't you a little curious?"

She was. But also afraid. What if she looked terrible?

He squeezed her hand. "Trust me. You look terrific." He stepped back. "After all, I'm a great photographer."

His mocking tone made her laugh, breaking the tension between them. "All right. I'll come over tonight. About nine?"

"Good." He picked up the folder of proof sheets. "I'll take these home and work on them there. Where there aren't so many distractions."

She laughed again. "You do that. In the meantime, maybe *I* can get some work done."

"Yeah. Put that fertile imagination of yours to work coming up with a sexy angle on barges and oil refineries." He went to the door and opened it. "See you later."

She sank behind her desk, weak-kneed in the aftermath of their lovemaking. She wasn't sorry for what she'd just done, but she knew she had just made her life a hell of a lot more complicated.

The old Glynna would have run from these kinds of complications. The new, improved version was determined to find a way to work around them. One lesson Jake had taught her was that anything worth having deserved a little struggle, whether it was a career...or a man.

STACY STASHED her gym bag in the locker and looked around to get her bearings. It wasn't as upscale as the club she usually frequented, but that didn't surprise her. Her club catered mostly to women, with pastel walls and pop music. From what she'd seen so far, this place served a mostly male clientele who wanted a good workout without a lot of distractions.

She smiled and ran one finger along the neck of her

leotard. Today she had a very particular distraction in mind for a certain art director.

She picked up her towel and left the locker room, pausing at the entrance to the gym until she spotted Nick. He was over by the free weights. She made her way to the barbell stand next to him, selected a pair of ten-pound dumbbells and began doing shoulder presses, waiting for him to notice her.

Standing with her profile to him, she studied Nick in the mirror. The muscles of his arms knotted as he thrust upward with the barbell, veins standing out in relief, a sheen of sweat on his brow. Her stomach tightened in response to such raw masculinity.

She knew she was playing a dangerous game, but a deliciously sexy one. The day Nick had come into her office to talk about the photo-essay, she'd been stunned by her attraction to him. Maybe it was his gorgeous body and the way he carried himself, or his competitive edge she could identify with. Maybe it was only that it had been a long time since she'd been in a relationship and she needed someone.

She'd sensed he was equally drawn to her, but that was no surprise. The man was a player who never stayed with one woman long. Office gossip had it that he preferred young, usually wealthy, socialites. Stacy had met his type before, and their multiple character flaws were enough to turn her off. But Nick was different. Despite everything bad she knew about him, one look into his honey-brown eyes and her temperature shot up.

She'd gone along with his not-so-subtle verbal teasing that day in her office, then decided to take things a step further. Why not play the game a little longer and see where it led? Nick wasn't the kind of man a woman could trust for the future, but he might be a pleasant interlude for the present.

"Stacy?" He sat up and grinned at her in the mirror. "I didn't know you worked out here."

"I'm thinking of joining. I have one of those trial memberships." She traded the ten-pound weight for fifteen and began doing bicep curls.

He selected twenty-pound weights and stood beside her to work on his forearms. "Jake showed me some of the shots he took at the ship channel. Awesome stuff."

She laughed. "The sexy side of the ship channel. It sounds ridiculous."

"Not if Glynna does half as good a job with the article as Jake did with the photos."

"Can you believe he took her to a strip joint?" She paused, the weights dangling from her hands. "Glynna McCormick? She doesn't seem the type."

"Sometimes the cool ones are the hottest when you get them alone." His eyes met hers in the mirror.

She looked away. "I supposed you consider yourself an expert."

"I know a thing or two about women."

"Hah!" She replaced the weights in the stand and shook out her arms. "You may know their bodies, but you don't have a clue about their minds."

"I might surprise you. A man who isn't interested in women's minds only wants to date dumb sex kittens." He continued to raise and lower the weight, muscles flexing and relaxing. The back of his gray T-shirt was wet with a triangle of sweat, and his hair was plastered to the back of his neck. Stripped of his expensive suits, he looked even more masculine, earthier. Here was a man she could imagine herself with. Peeling off those sweaty clothes to reveal the body underneath...

"I thought a dumb sex kitten was every man's ideal woman." She walked over to the weight bench and lowered herself to do tricep dips.

"Maybe some men. But after a certain age, a man appreciates a woman with a spectacular mind to go with a spectacular body." In the mirror, she saw his gaze shift to her breasts, which were thrust in front of her by the position of the exercise.

She paused at the bottom of the dip, holding herself still, muscles trembling. "Have you thought of a subject for the photo-essay?"

He turned to face her. "Does this mean you've agreed to put it in?"

"I'll consider it." She raised herself up onto the bench and sat, stretching her arms out in front of her.

He grinned and turned to face the mirror again, though he still watched her reflection. "Have you figured out what you want from me in return?"

She could think of a few things. She raised her chin. "Do you still think the visual is more important than words?"

"The visual creates a visceral reaction in people. An immediate response."

"Such as?"

"Such as I'm getting a hard-on right now, watching you." His look was taunting, daring her to be shocked.

She hid a smile. His arousal hadn't escaped her notice. The sight of the thick ridge at the fly of his shorts had fueled her own desire. "But words can be powerful, too. What if I told you I wanted to have sex with you?"

She heard his breath catch, saw his smile waver. He turned to face her. "Are you serious?"

"What did I tell you? Those words created an immediate response, didn't they?" She let her gaze drop to his crotch.

"Answer my question."

She stood and picked up her towel. "I guess that's for you to find out."

She sauntered past him, hips swaying.

"Where are you going?" he demanded.

"I'm going home to take a shower."

She heard the clank of weights being dropped into place, then his footsteps as he caught up with her. "Wait for me."

She turned and held up her hand. "No. Don't follow me."

He frowned. "You just said you wanted to get it on with me."

"No, I said you had to find out if that's what I really wanted."

"What kind of a game are you playing here?"

She allowed herself a smile. "I think it could be a very interesting one. If you play it right." Before he could answer, she turned and hurried toward the women's locker room. Her skin tingled with awareness of him watching her, and her nerves hummed with arousal. Inviting Nick home with her now would be too easy. She planned to make him squirm a little. To make him want her as much as she was beginning to want him.

11

WEDNESDAY-NIGHT DINNER together was an established tradition for Glynna and her father. For as long as she could remember, every Wednesday evening she would dress in her Sunday best and sit across from him at the downtown steakhouse he favored. When she was a little girl, the dinners had made her feel grown-up; she was usually the only child in the place. When she was a teenager she had suffered through the meals, where the conversation often seemed to consist of a litany of ways she should be improving herself.

Now that she was older, the meals had assumed a formal familiarity. Most often, they talked about work or current events. As if they were casual acquaintances.

"How is the ship channel piece coming along?" Gordon asked tonight when the waiter had served their salads.

"It's going very well." She picked at her lettuce. "There's a lot more to the area than I thought."

"I'm glad to hear it." He sliced into a chunk of tomato. "Good solid reporting. That's what our readers want. Not fluff pieces on sex resorts."

"I don't know. Sometimes people just want to relax and be entertained." She set down her fork and met his gaze. "I thought the piece on La Paloma turned out very well."

"Hmmmph. Your talent is wasted on trash like that. It's bad enough Stacy assigned it to you, but to send that long-haired photographer with you."

She stiffened. "Jake is very talented. He's the best photographer on staff."

"That doesn't make up for disrespect and arrogance. There are hundreds of gifted bums in this world. They find out soon enough talent doesn't take the place of dedication and hard work."

"Jake does work hard. He freelances and has a gallery show opening in a few days."

He waited to answer while he chewed his salad. "I'm well aware that he considers himself an artist. Give me a good solid photojournalist any day." He regarded her as he speared another forkful of lettuce. "And I don't appreciate the way he looks at you."

The skin at the back of her neck prickled, and a thrill shot through her. "How does he look at me?"

"Not the way a father likes to see that kind of man look at his daughter." He shoved salad into his mouth and munched vigorously.

She fought back a blush, and a smile of pleasure. So she hadn't misjudged Jake's interest in her. "I'm sure you're imagining things. Jake and I are too different to ever have a serious relationship." But a temporary one was a different story.... This time she did let her smile show.

"Exactly the reason you should avoid him. He's like too many young people these days. They don't take anything seriously."

"Oh, please." For once she let her exasperation show. "You sound like you're a hundred years old." She tried for a teasing tone. "Don't tell me you don't still know how to have fun."

He frowned. "I enjoy my work. Few enough people can say that."

"And I enjoy my work, too." At least most of it. "But other things in life are just as important. Like relationships."

"I have friends. Don't make me out to be some bitter old man."

Not bitter exactly. But certainly unbending. "What about women?" With a shock she realized she couldn't remember her father ever being seriously involved with a woman since her mother's death. "Haven't you ever thought of remarrying?"

He compressed his lips into a thin line and pushed aside his salad. "I was fortunate enough to love one very special woman. I seriously doubt I would be so lucky twice."

She started to object, but he cut her off. "I am perfectly aware that I am a stern, somewhat unemotional man. Some would say cold. That is my nature and I don't apologize for it. For whatever reason, your mother saw past that. We were happy together and I am content to live with the memory of that."

But a memory doesn't keep a person warm at night, she thought.

"What about you? You're an attractive young woman. I assume there have been…that there are…relationships with men. Though so far you have been discreet."

She flushed. "I've dated some. Not seriously."

He sipped from a glass of iced tea. "Are you seeing anyone at the moment?"

She shifted in her seat, avoiding his eyes. To think she had once longed for him to take a more personal interest in her life! "Nothing serious." Though her father would probably think differently if he knew she and Jake were sleeping together.

The waiter arrived with their steaks. She was grateful for the interruption. But her father picked up the thread of the conversation. "Stay away from Jake Dawson."

"What makes you think I'm interested in Jake?" Had someone seen him go into her office this afternoon? Had they noted the closed door and reported back to her father?

"I know he's the kind of man women act foolish about. I trust you have more sense."

"You've certainly raised me to be sensible." And what had that gotten her so far? Lonely nights and grim prospects for the future. Her relationship with Jake, temporary though it had to be, was the start of changing that.

Her father sliced into his steak. "Good. Now how are you coming with that revenue report I asked for?"

She bit back a sigh. Work again. Dull, unemotional, safe. "I'll have it for you by the end of the week."

"Excellent. I know I can always count on you."

At one time, she'd have lived on such praise for weeks. Now it left a dull ache around her heart. She wanted him to think of her as more than competent and obedient. He wasn't the kind of man who spoke words of love, but would it be too much to hope that he wanted her to be, not just successful, but happy?

JAKE STOOD BACK and surveyed his apartment. He'd spent the afternoon cleaning for Glynna's visit. Not that he was a big slob, but he was too busy most of the time to notice dust and she struck him as the kind of woman who kept things spotless. He didn't want her turned off the minute she walked in the door. He'd even bought a vanilla scented candle and lit it, hoping to drown out the smell of darkroom chemicals.

He shook his head. He'd never thought he'd see the day when Glynna McCormick would be coming over to his place, but then, after what had happened in her office this afternoon he was through trying to predict her behavior. His stomach tightened at the thought of her perched on the edge of her desk, her face transformed by passion. The moment had been incredibly erotic, and moving, too. It couldn't have been easy for her to reveal herself to him that way. But why had she done it?

A woman like her could find any number of men to satisfy her lust. She had the looks and background to attract most of the city's movers and shakers. Had she fixed on Jake because she knew him and he was available? Was it because of what had happened between them on La Paloma? What exactly *had* happened there? They'd both agreed to a single weekend of fun, but neither one of them had been very successful at putting it behind them.

He'd be the first to admit he and Glynna had more than a casual connection. That weekend with her had touched him more deeply than he liked to admit. But he still thought continuing to see her was a bad idea. He was going away and that would hurt her. Never mind his own pain at leaving her behind.

He'd tried to break it off, but when she'd started unbuttoning her blouse there in her office he'd lost the last bit of willpower he'd been clinging to. What the hell did it matter what happened next week when she was offering him heaven now?

The doorbell rang and he flinched, took one last look around the apartment and went to answer it. "Hello there." He greeted her with a smile and held open the door. She was wearing a sleeveless white dress, made out of some expensive, clingy fabric. Her skin looked golden against it, her hair like silk around her face. As she moved past, he caught the scent of her perfume, sweet and sensuous.

"I'm sorry I'm late. Dinner took longer than I expected."

"How is Gordon?" He hoped for her sake the old man was nicer in private than he was in public.

"Crotchety." She smiled. "He spent most of the evening warning me to stay away from you."

He frowned. "Why? Did someone see us together and say something to him?"

She shook her head. "I don't think so. I guess he's just feeling…protective."

"I can't say I blame him. It's pretty obvious I'm not the type of man a father wants hanging around his daughter." He caressed her bare shoulder. "Aside from the fact that he barely tolerates me, I'm definitely not the blue-blood society type."

"I'm thinking the society type wouldn't make me scream the way you do." She stood on tiptoe to kiss him, desire knifing through him as her tongue darted into his mouth. She pressed against him, her body silently communicating with his. She was so hot. How had he ever thought her cold?

With some effort, he drew away from her. He didn't want to rush things. He wanted to make love to her half the night, discovering all the ways they could please each other. "Would you like some wine?"

"That would be nice."

While he went to pour the drinks, she looked around the living room. "You have a nice place."

"Thanks. The owners hired me to photograph the complex for a sales brochure. I liked it so much, I ended up signing a lease."

"Did you take this photo?"

He looked up from the bar and saw that she'd paused before a black-and-white shot of a Vietnamese fisherman. The man, his face weathered by years of sun and salt, looked directly into the camera, a thin cigarette curling smoke between his fingers. "That's the photo that won me the scholarship to Rice."

She gazed at other photos: a line of stevedores, bent under their burdens, marching up the gangplank of a ship. The Houston skyline at night. An Alabama-Coushatta Indian hunting in the Big Thicket. She moved on to the leather sofa, trailing her hands along the back.

He handed her a glass of wine. "Is something wrong?"

She flushed. "I guess I'm a little nervous…anxious to see the photos you took of me."

He sat on the sofa and picked up an envelope from the coffee table. "Come sit down and we'll take a look."

The leather of the sofa creaked as she settled beside him, almost, but not quite touching him. He wanted to pull her close, but held back. What if she hated the photos? The evening would end before it began.

He opened the envelope and slid out the first shot. In it, Glynna lay supine, arms up, shielding her eyes. The curve of her mouth was visible, a satisfied half smile hinting at what must have come before. The bright light shadowed the hollow of her throat, the valleys between her breasts and thighs, the rumpled sheets surrounding her. The skin of her breasts and stomach and thighs gleamed like marble. Her limbs looked long and supple, her curves soft and feminine.

It was an incredibly erotic image. He'd gotten a hard-on developing it, remembering how her skin had felt, how her mouth had tasted. He spent hours dodging the shadows, softening the contrast from stark to tender, until the picture resembled a painting as much as a photograph.

She held the photo for a long moment, saying nothing. Finally, he could stand it no more. "What do you think?"

She looked at him, eyes bright with tears. His stomach knotted. "What's wrong?" Did she hate it? How could she?

"You made me look so beautiful," she whispered.

Confused, he touched her arm. "But you are beautiful."

She shook her head. "Not like this. You made me look how I feel when I'm with you."

He pulled her close and kissed her cheek, tasting salt. He wanted to comfort her though he didn't understand her sorrow. "You know they say an artist is only as good as his subject."

Her smile cheered him. She kissed his mouth. "Thank you. I never would have dreamed I could look like this."

"I'll always think of you this way." He kissed her again and hugged her, the photo pressed between them. When she pulled away to lay the picture on the table, he took her hand. "Let's go to the bedroom."

He led her into the room, where the bedside lamps cast soft pools of light across the black satin comforter of his king-size bed. He dropped her hand and went to turn on the stereo. Soft jazz swelled around them.

"Miles Davis," she identified the trumpet player.

"I didn't know before today you liked jazz," he said.

She nodded. "It's very…sensuous music." She bent to stroke the comforter. "I've never been in a man's bedroom before. Can you believe it?"

He moved toward her, but she avoided him, skirting around to the other side of the bed, refusing to look at him. Her nervousness touched him. He'd never met a woman who was such a mix of contradictions: bold one moment, shy the next; wild enough to seduce him and reserved enough to blush at the slightest provocation.

He sat on the edge of the bed and patted the spot next to him. "Come sit down."

She did so, her hands in her lap. He took her chin and turned her head until she was looking at him. "Do you trust me?" he asked.

She hesitated, then nodded. "You've never given me cause not to."

"Then lie down." He gently pressed her back against the mattress. "Relax. We're going to enjoy ourselves."

She lay down, and brought her feet up until she was stretched out, her head propped up on a pillow. He leaned over and kissed her again, opening his mouth to taste her fully, his tongue teasing, stroking, exploring. She responded, putting her arms around him and drawing him nearer. He caressed her breast through the fabric of her dress and felt her nipple rise up to meet his hand.

His mouth still on hers, he undid the first button at the front of the dress. She reached for his shirt, but he gently pushed her hand away. "No. Let me do the work."

He undressed her slowly, flicking open the buttons one at a time, his fingertips grazing the warm flesh between her breasts, across her ribs, down her stomach. He eased the fabric aside, savoring each inch of her as it was revealed. Her skin glowed in the light, soft and golden. He traced the line of her ribs and outlined the dip of her belly button. She watched him, her eyes dark, her breathing shallow.

He unsnapped her bra and pushed it aside, brushing his hands across her breasts as he did so. The skin around her nipples tightened, and she pressed herself into his palm. "You like it when I touch you there, don't you?" he asked.

She nodded and moistened her lips. "I love it when you lick me there."

"Like this?" He flicked his tongue across each nipple in turn, smiling as her body jerked against him. "Or like this?" He surrounded her with his lips, drawing as much of her breast as possible into his mouth, scrubbing his tongue across her erect nipple. She moaned and he increased the pace and pressure, his hand splayed across her stomach, holding her down as she arched toward him.

He paid the same attention to her other breast, sliding his hand down, beneath the silk of her panties, burying his finger in her damp curls. She spread her legs for him, inviting him inside her, but he only cupped her lightly before moving up again. He wanted to make her wait, to draw out the anticipation a little longer.

He helped her out of her dress and underwear, then moved back, leaving her lying on the bed naked, her body still wet where he had kissed and suckled. She watched him as he took a step back from the bed.

"What are you doing?" she asked.

"I'm getting undressed." He undid the top button of his shirt. His usual approach was to tear off his clothes as fast as he could, but he stuck to his plan to slow things down tonight. As the saxophone moaned softly in the background, he opened his shirt carefully, one button at a time, his gaze locked to Glynna's. She watched him, eyes dark and dilated, lips slightly parted, breathing heavily.

He shrugged off the shirt and let it fall to the floor, then rolled his shoulders, the muscles of his chest and arms flexing. Her breathing became more labored and he smiled. He'd never stripped like this for a woman before; he was surprised how much of a turn-on it was for him, watching her.

He smoothed his hand across his stomach, down beneath the waistband of his pants. His erection strained at his fly. Eyes still locked to Glynna's, telegraphing how much he wanted her, he reached for his belt. Heart thudding in time to the music, he slowly pulled it free and lowered the zipper of his pants.

He shed trousers and socks quickly, his impatience to lie beside her growing. But he made himself stand before her a moment, the thick outline of his erection obvious in his briefs. She raised herself up on her elbows. "Put on your chaps," she said.

He hesitated, one hand at the waistband of his briefs, about to pull them down. "What?"

"Take off your briefs and put on your motorcycle chaps."

He grinned. "So you like my chaps."

"Don't tell me you're oblivious to the fact that they draw attention to your crotch and your backside."

He laughed. "I didn't know you were looking."

"Oh, women look. We just aren't as obvious about it as men." She focused again on his bulging groin. "I want to see you naked except for those chaps."

SHE HALF EXPECTED him to refuse her request. He'd made a point of taking charge this evening and the chaps obviously weren't part of his plan. But after a second's hesitation, he retrieved the chaps from his closet and stripped off his briefs.

The dark leather of the chaps made a stark contrast to his pale skin, and hugged his ass cheeks. She wanted to put her hands there, to feel his muscles bunch as he thrust into her.

When he turned around, she sucked in her breath at the sight of his erection framed by the leather. He was very hard, the head of his penis tapping against his firm belly. "Come here." She beckoned him.

He moved toward her, his erection jutting out before him. She heard the scrape of the leather against his thighs, and saw her own desire reflected back at her in his eyes.

When he reached the bed, she sat up and took hold of him, her fingers feathering lightly against his balls before wrapping more firmly around his cock. He grunted. "Careful."

"Oh, I'll be very careful." She bent and kissed the tip, tasting the moisture there, hearing the sharp intake of his breath as she stroked her tongue along the shaft. Not wanting to push him too far, she kissed his thigh, smoothing her tongue along the edge of the leather, her hair falling across his erection, brushing his skin.

He nudged her shoulder. "You're supposed to be relaxing," he said.

She laughed. "I wouldn't call what I've been doing relaxing." She lay back and looked up at him. "I'm on fire for you, don't you know that?"

He knelt beside her. "And I'm just as hot for you." He kissed her mouth again, a deep, quenching kiss, then slid down her body, pausing briefly to lap at her aching nipples before laying a trail of kisses down her stomach to the damp curls between her legs. He teased her, planting light, feathering kisses at the juncture of each thigh and across her labia, until she was moaning and thrusting against him, impatient for release of this tension within her.

He rested his hand on her stomach, a gentling motion. "What do you want?" he asked.

"You know what I want."

He smiled. "You have to learn to ask for it."

She wet her lips, irritated that he was asking this of her, but also knowing he was right. Wasn't her desire to be her own woman what had brought them together? "I want you to make me come," she said at last.

"How?" He was breathing heavily, his mouth resting against her thigh.

"I…I want you to suck my clit. And put your fingers inside me."

She had barely finished speaking before he was doing as she asked. She felt a thrill that she'd said the words, that she'd spoken up for herself as she did too seldom.

With his tongue and mouth and fingers, he stoked the fires within her. He caressed and stroked, faster, then slower, building up the sensation within her, making her wait, but making the wait worth her while. She thrust toward him, straining, wanting to plead with him to let her come, but loving what he was doing too much to ask him to stop.

She came hard, bucking against him, her scream soaring above the music. His fingers still in her, he raised up and reached for the box of condoms on the bedside table. He ripped open the packet with his teeth and sheathed himself, then eased into her.

The pressure of him inside her began another spiral of arousal. The leather of his chaps rubbed against her thighs as he thrust in and out of her, and she reached around to grasp his buttocks, burying her fingers in his firm flesh. With a last hard thrust, he came also, his muscles clenching beneath her hand.

Still keeping inside her, he rolled over, taking her with him. They faced each other, eyes open, saying nothing, waiting for hearts to slow and breathing to return to normal. He stroked one finger down her cheek. "You're really something, you know that?"

"I don't think I knew it before." She rested her head in the hollow of his shoulders. "But thanks to you, I think I'm beginning to find out."

12

GLYNNA DIDN'T REMEMBER how she got to work the next morning. She had a vague recollection of stumbling home in the wee hours and taking a quick shower before dashing to the office, but the drive there had been spent reliving every wonderful moment of the night before.

When Jake had put those chaps on for her, her feeble efforts to be a tough, live-for-the-moment gal had collapsed around her ankles. Her emotions were as exposed as her body, and she didn't even care. She had fallen head-over-heels, hearts-and-flowers in love with Jake. The knowledge made her giddy and dizzy, and she couldn't wipe the smile off her face.

"Good night! What happened to you?"

Glynna looked up to find Stacy standing in her doorway. She straightened and tried to assume an innocent expression. "Stacy, come in. What can I do for you?"

"How about answering my question?" Stacy strode across the room and perched on the edge of the sofa across from Glynna's desk. "There's only two things that can put a smile like that on a woman's face—good drugs or fantastic sex. So unless you're popping pills for some mysterious injury, you'd better fess up."

Glynna cursed her propensity for blushing as heat rose to her face. "I'm not taking painkillers," she said. "Or anything else."

"I knew it!" Stacy crowed. "It's sex. And about damn time, if I may say so."

Glynna shot a worried look toward the door. "Not so loud," she pleaded. "What if my father hears you?"

"What if he does?" She settled back against the love seat. "Might do him some good to think of you as a grown-up woman."

Where had she heard those words before? "Honestly, does everyone think I'm so pathetic?" she asked.

"Not pathetic." Stacy shook her head. "Gordon's the one I feel sorry for really. He's going to have a rude awakening someday." She sat forward again, elbows on her knees. "But stop trying to change the subject. Who's the lucky guy? Anyone I know?"

Glynna's blush deepened. Did Jake think he was lucky to be with her? She hoped so. "I can't tell you," she said.

"Can't tell me?" Stacy's eyes widened and she lowered her voice. "Why not? Is he married?"

"No!" Glynna plucked a paper clip from her desk tray and began unbending it. "I...I don't want to say his name. Not yet." Sharing what she and Jake had with someone else right now—even Stacy—might spoil it. Besides, she wasn't sure of Jake's feelings for her. Certainly, he agreed what they had between them was special, but what did that mean to a man, anyway? Especially a guy like Jake, who'd had many relationships with women. For Glynna, this was a once-in-a-lifetime event. Maybe for Jake it wasn't so unique.

"Don't look like that! What did I say?" Stacy stared at her, clearly concerned.

The paper clip broke in Glynna's hand and she tossed it aside. "Look like what? I'm fine."

"You looked like someone just cut up all your credit cards." Stacy smiled. "Okay, I won't press. But I hope whoever he is, it works out for y'all." She stood. "You deserve to be happy, girlfriend. And if that man of yours doesn't treat you right, you let me know and I'll make him see the error of his ways."

She laughed. "Stacy, I don't think you're nearly as tough as you like to pretend."

"No?" Stacy glanced from side to side, then lowered her voice. "Don't tell anyone. It would totally ruin my image."

When Stacy was gone, Glynna booted up her computer and tried to concentrate on work, but her mind refused to focus on anything but Jake. She checked her watch. They'd been apart five hours and already she missed him. How pathetic was that?

Sighing, she slipped on her shoes and stood. Maybe if she walked down to the photographers' workroom and talked to him that would be enough to allow her to get some work done. That is, if he'd even come in yet.

Activity on the art side of the magazine's offices was muted this morning. The photographers and graphic artists tended to keep later hours than the journalists, and reported to their desks whenever mood and schedule dictated, sometimes working at home, or in the middle of the night. She was relieved to find Jake in his office. He stood with his back to her, bent over a light box.

Heat curled through her as her gaze swept over his long legs and jean-clad backside. The only thing better than Jake in jeans was Jake naked…or maybe wearing chaps.

He turned suddenly, startling her. "Oh, hi, Jake. I, uh, I stopped by to see how you're doing."

"I'm fine." He picked up the proof sheet and dropped it on his desk, not looking at her. "You okay?"

"Oh, yeah. I'm great." She moved closer, suddenly unsure how to act. Would it be bad office etiquette to hurl herself over the desk and throw her arms around him? She settled for resting her hands on the polished wood and leaning toward him. "I was wondering if you'd like to have lunch with me today."

He tapped out something on his computer keyboard and shook his head. "No, I'm really busy today."

She frowned. Would it kill him to look at her? "Oh. Okay. What about dinner?"

He glanced at her then, a brief, apologetic look. "I'm sorry, but I'm really swamped right now." He returned his attention to his computer.

She stepped back and continued to watch him, waiting for him to say something else…to *do* something else. After the night they'd had together, how could he possibly go about business as usual?

He glanced up at her again. "Did you need something else?"

I need you to explain why you're acting so weird. She took a deep breath. "What's going on?" she asked.

He straightened. "Nothing's going on. I'm busy, that's all."

He was *busy.* "Okay. Fine." She got the message.

This was male code for "back off." What had happened between them last night had apparently been one-sided. It had been just sex for him all along. She backed toward the door. "I'll let you get back to work then."

She turned and was almost in the corridor when he stopped her. "Look, we'll have dinner soon," he said. "I'll call you."

She nodded, not bothering to turn around. Why let him see how hurt she was? "Yeah. Call me."

She hurried away, before he could say anything else to make things worse. Jake wanted dinner for one night, while she wanted to sit across the table from him every night for the rest of her life. They'd been going along so great, then she had to screw it up by falling in love!

NICK DIDN'T KNOW what to think of Stacy's on-again, off-again flirtation with him. One minute she'd be giving him come-hither looks from across the room, and the next she'd assume her all-business persona and discuss the merits of various illustrations for some back-of-the-book fluff piece. She obviously enjoyed keeping him off balance. After every disturbing encounter with her, he swore he was through playing her games. Then he'd find himself watching her walk down the hall, those gorgeous legs of hers encased in sheer hose, skirt pulled tight over her perfect ass…and he'd be under her spell again, determined to break through her reserve and get to her the way she got to him.

So when she called to schedule a time to look at the preliminary layout for the next issue of *Texas Style,* he suggested they meet in his office. Maybe he'd do better on his own turf. *He'd* be the one to keep her guessing his motives this time.

But then she walked into his office and any plan he'd had to play it cool evaporated in a rush of heat. She was wearing a red leather suit, with a fitted cropped jacket and a short skirt. It was the kind of expensive, designer outfit that screamed sex and success, and was intended to awe and intimidate. Nick fell prey to both emotions, but quickly regained control. So she wanted to play rough, did she? He was game. The thought of taking that suit off, slowly, made him more determined than ever to cut through the crap and get down to business. And it had nothing to do with art or letters and everything to do with the attraction that set off sparks between them.

"I can't believe they pulled it off," she said as she scanned proof sheets of the photos for the story on the ship channel. She held up a page that featured a shot of a dark-skinned woman in a gold bikini sunning on the deck of a yacht while the rusty hulk of a freighter loomed in the background. "They've actually made the ship channel seem exotic, vibrant and even sexy."

"Wait until you see what I'm thinking of using for the cover shot." He opened a file and took out an oversized glossy and slid it across the desk. The stacks of a petrochemical plant jutted skyward in the foreground, while in the distance, the garish neon of a strip club flashed Live! Nude! Girls!

A hint of a smile played about Stacy's lips. "You don't think it's too…phallic?"

"You said you wanted sexy."

The smile bloomed fully now. "Gordon will have a conniption."

"Aren't you worried he'll call you on the carpet again?"

"I don't care if he does." But her voice didn't quite carry through the bravado of her words. "The latest circulation figures came in this morning."

He settled one hip onto the corner of his desk. "And?"

"And twenty-five hundred subscribers have canceled their subscriptions in protest over the Paloma Island story."

He frowned. "That doesn't sound like anything to be crowing about."

Her smile widened. "We also have almost *four thousand* new subscribers. *The Chronicle* wants to do a piece on us for their weekly business review and *Masthead* is interested in a feature for their upcoming issue."

His grin matched hers. "Even Gordon should be happy with that news."

"I haven't told him yet. I'm waiting for the right moment." She bent over the layout again.

"You like to do that, don't you?"

"Do what?" She turned a page, eyes scanning the text.

"You like to make men wait."

"Now why would you say that?"

As if she didn't know. Since that exchange in the gym he'd been alternately furious and fascinated. He didn't like being manipulated, but there was something else going on with Stacy. Something…different from any other relationship he'd had with a woman.

Socially, economically and even physically, they

were well-matched. Usually he preferred relationships where he had the upper hand. He didn't want to compete with the women he dated, and yet there was something exhilarating, erotic even, about matching wits with a woman who was as strong as he was.

"I tried to call you last night," he said. He'd let the phone ring a dozen times, hoping she'd pick up.

"I wasn't answering my phone."

Because she'd known it was him? Or because she was with someone else? His jaw tightened at the thought.

She leaned over his desk again, turning pages. Her blond hair fell forward, obscuring her face and framing the cleavage revealed by the low neckline of her jacket. He imagined running his tongue along the sloping sides of her breasts. Would she sigh or moan at his touch?

"Enjoying the view?" Her eyes danced with laughter as she caught his gaze and held it. As if to taunt him, she traced the plunging collar of the jacket with one red-tipped nail.

"Since you went to so much trouble to display it for me, yes." He straightened and walked around the desk to stand beside her.

"You think I wore this outfit just for you? Please!" She rolled her eyes.

He stood close, almost but not quite touching her. He wanted her to be the one to reach for him. "Didn't you?" He let his eyes drift over her, the tension building between them. He suppressed a surge of triumph when she looked away.

"You're delusional," she said.

"Admit it. You get off on teasing me. The question is, what do you really want?"

She thrust her shoulders back and assumed her superior smile once more. "You tell me. You're the man who supposedly knows so much about women's minds."

He leaned closer, his lips almost brushing hers. If she even took a deep breath, he'd have her. "You know you want me," he growled.

Desire flared in her eyes, the pupils dilating. "Maybe I only get off on teasing you."

"A woman like you needs more than that." He clenched his hands at his side, fighting the craving to pull her into his arms. "You *want* more."

She cocked one eyebrow. "But what *exactly* do I want?"

The question caught him off guard. Again. "Care to give me any hints?"

"When you find the right approach, I promise you'll know."

She stepped back, putting distance between them.

He inhaled, reminding himself this was his office and the door was open. He couldn't very well lay her back across the desk and show her the approach he thought she needed. "And in the meantime?"

She smiled and turned back to the proof sheets. "In the meantime, we have a magazine to get out."

She was a piece of work! What did she want from him? And why was he going to so much trouble to find out?

JAKE GUNNED the bike around the curve, trying to blow away the fog that seemed to spread through his brain these days. A fog filled with images of Glynna. He hadn't seen her other than in passing. It had been a week since he'd ignored her in his office the morning after she'd spent the night at his apartment.

He'd winced at the memory. He'd handled it badly, making those lame excuses about work when all he'd really wanted was to pull her into his arms and kiss her until they were both breathless. But there was no point in that, was there? No point in taking things any further between them. Every minute they spent together would only make the break that much harder when time came for him to leave.

Logic told him that, but the rest of his brain refused to pay attention. He couldn't stop thinking about her. Two days ago, he'd ruined a whole roll of negatives when he'd opened the cannister before they'd been through the developing solution.

So much for his plan to get his thinking back on track. He told himself he was doing the right thing, trying to keep it casual and avoid hurting her, but in the predawn hours when he lay awake and admitted the truth to himself, he knew there was nothing casual about the way Glynna made him feel. All the more reason to keep his distance.

Especially now. He could feel the letter from New York in the inside pocket of his jacket. A friend from school, Ernie Shiffel, had written, offering to introduce him to some influential people in the city—art dealers, gallery owners, editors and critics. People who could help him get started in the New York art photography world.

This was the break he'd been waiting for. He couldn't let anything distract him from it. He needed to put together a killer portfolio, make travel arrangements, get his finances in order. He didn't have time for a relationship. Especially not with Glynna. She was too…complicated. Too…distracting. Too…difficult to let go of whenever she was near.

When Stacy had called this morning to ask him to stop by her office, he had almost balked. But the money from *Texas Style* was too good to pass up. He couldn't afford to quit yet. The thing to do would be to get in and out of the building as quickly as possible, and to avoid running into Glynna.

Stacy was waiting for him in her office when he arrived. He froze in the doorway when he spotted Glynna, seated in a chair in front of Stacy's desk. "Hello, Jake," she said, her smile so genuine and welcoming it made his heart clench.

Her affection for him was written all over her face. It frightened him, seeing how much she cared. He was used to harder women, the kind who hid their feelings.

Stacy must have noticed the look, too. She glanced at Glynna, then at Jake, questions in her eyes. Ignoring her, he strode across the room and sat in the only other chair, next to Glynna. He watched her out of the corner of his eye, avoiding looking at her head-on. He didn't want to feel any more of a louse than he already did.

"What's up?" he asked Stacy. "I've got tons of work piling up."

The editor handed them each copies of the latest issue of *Texas Style*. "Congratulations on the great job you did on the ship channel piece. Gordon is very pleased."

He frowned at the mention of the publisher's name. "Has he actually looked at the piece?" He couldn't imagine Gordon being "pleased" with interviews with strippers and photos of sunbathing tourists.

Stacy looked down at the desk. "No. Not exactly. I told him it turned out well and he said he'd take my word for it."

"His exact phrase was 'even those two can't screw up a piece on shipping and industry,'" Glynna said. "And he's so happy about the new circulation figures, he's decided to let Stacy go back to assigning stories."

Stacy's smile was full-blown now. "He agrees a whole series spotlighting different areas of the city would be a terrific idea."

Glynna made a face. "You mean, 'the sexy side of the museum district'?"

"Not just sex, but what you did in the ship channel story." Stacy tapped the magazine. "Take something we're familiar with—or not so familiar with as the case may be—and show the city within the city. If there's a certain…sensuality to the piece, so be it. Despite what some may think, we're not here to cater solely to prurient interests."

Jake shifted in his chair. "Okay, but what does this have to do with me?"

"I want you to work with Glynna on the next story in the series, a feature on Houston underground—the tunnel system under downtown."

He had to admit it was a good choice. There were people who'd lived in the Bayou City for years and never visited the maze of tunnels underneath downtown. And it would be fun to explore the area with Glynna. Too much fun. He couldn't risk what might happen if he spent time alone with her, working or not. "It's a great idea, but I have to pass."

"What do you mean?" Glynna stared at him, obviously stunned.

"Sorry, but I've got too many other things on my plate right now. You'll have to find another photographer for this one." He sensed Glynna's eyes on him but forced himself not to look at her. "I'm too swamped to take on another project."

Frown lines etched a vee between Stacy's brows. She looked at them both for a long moment, then nodded. "All right. I'll have the new hire, Jason Burke, or maybe Missy Thorpe, a freelancer, go with you, Glynna."

She said nothing. Jake shoved out of the chair. His chest felt tight. He had to get out of there. "I'd better be going."

Stacy nodded and he headed for the door. But before he could reach it, Glynna darted past him. She shoved open the door and raced into the hall. He stared after her, feeling sick. What had he done now?

"Jake, what's going on?" Stacy came up behind him.

He shook his head. "I don't know." That was the truth, at least. He didn't know where he stood with Glynna, or where he wanted to stand. They should have left their feelings for each other back on the island. Bringing them into the real world made everything too complicated.

"Are you and Glynna…? I mean…have the two of you been dating?" Stacy asked.

He shook his head. "Not exactly." They'd skipped right over the dating phase and gone right to bed. It had seemed like a good idea at the time, but now he wondered. Despite her modern attitudes about some things, Glynna was really an old-fashioned girl. She deserved a more traditional approach to relationships.

"I don't understand—" Stacy began.

"Neither do I. Listen, I have to go."

Once in the hallway, he stopped to try to determine which way Glynna would have gone. He needed to talk to her, to clear things up between them.

He headed toward her office, but when he passed the door to the ladies' room he stopped and turned back. If Glynna had been truly upset, there was a good chance she'd have headed there.

Hoping his hunch was right, he checked to make sure the hall was empty, then ducked inside the women's restroom.

The first thing that struck him was how pink everything was. Pink walls. A pink flowered sofa in a sitting alcove. What did women do that they needed a sofa in the restroom? There was a flower arrangement on the counter between the sinks, and dispensers of hand lotion next to the soap. The men's facilities were bare and utilitarian in contrast.

He cautiously peeked his head around the wall that divided the toilets from the rest of the room. Glynna was slumped against a stall, dabbing at her eyes with a tissue. When she saw Jake, she straightened. "Jake! What are you doing in here?"

"I came to see if you were all right." He shoved his

hands in the pockets of his jeans. It was either that or reach for her.

"I'm fine. Why wouldn't I be?" She attempted to hide the hand holding the tissue behind her back, and blinked rapidly, as if that would erase the redness in her eyes.

"Look, I'm sorry I've been blowing you off lately." He took a step toward her, wanting to close not only the physical gap, but the emotional rift between them. "I know I've been a dick, but I can explain."

"You don't owe me any explanations." She sniffed and the tissue appeared to dab at her eyes again. "I told you before, I don't have any claims on you."

"I don't think two people can experience the things we've experienced in bed together and not feel some kinds of ties," he said. "I know we agreed to keep it casual between us, but it had already gone beyond that, at least for me, after that first night."

She stared at him, lips parted. "What are you trying to say?"

He swallowed hard. He wasn't good with words. He preferred pictures. People could make up their own minds about what he was trying to say in his photos. "I'm saying that, for whatever reason, you've affected me like no other woman. I can't stop thinking about you." He looked at the floor. "I can't stop wanting to be with you. But that's not a good thing for me."

"Why not?"

He reached into his jacket and took out the letter. "Read this. Then maybe you'll understand."

She took the single typewritten sheet from the envelope and scanned it. When she looked up at him again, she gave him a shaky smile. "He's inviting you to New York. It…it's what you've wanted, isn't it?"

He nodded. "But you see why I can't get involved with anyone right now. And since I can't keep it casual with you, I think it's better we don't see each other again." He closed the gap between them, unable to keep from touching her any longer. At the feel of his hand on her shoulder, she sagged against him, leaning her head on his chest.

"I don't know whether to be flattered you think so much of me, or furious that you don't want to see me again."

He smoothed his hand down her back, resisting the urge to slide lower, to cup her bottom. "I just think it's better if we keep our distance," he said. "I want to leave town believing we're still friends."

She raised her head to look at him, and her expression, trying to be brave, almost destroyed his resolve. "You'll always be my friend," she said. "And I want you to be happy in New York." The courage behind her words made his heart ache. It would have been so much easier if she'd railed at him and called him a selfish bastard. At least that was the truth, not these polite lies.

"I want you to be happy here." He didn't want to think about who she might be happy with, if it wasn't him. He squeezed her arm and pulled away. "It'll be for the best. You'll see."

"Sure." She turned away. "You'd better get out of the ladies' room before someone comes in."

"Right." He backed toward the door, eyes still on her. Was she really going to be okay?

She waved him away. "Go on. I'm going to freshen up a little."

He turned and walked away, but the sadness in her eyes remained fixed in his mind. He knew he'd done the right thing in breaking it off with her. Still, he felt like a big jerk. Glynna deserved a man who would be there for her in the long haul, something he couldn't guarantee. He didn't know where his ambitions would lead him or how long it would take to get there. But he did know he couldn't focus on work and a woman at the same time. "Single-minded" a professor had called him once, praising his hard work. Concentrating on one goal at a time had gotten him out of the oil-field ghetto, into college and the work he loved. He had everything he'd ever wanted, career-wise, within sight now, as long as he didn't let himself get distracted. Maybe later, when things were more settled for him, he and Glynna could hook up again. If she didn't hate him by then.

13

GLYNNA CHECKED her watch for the fifth time in ten minutes and stared at the front door of the Bank One building, the toe of her shoe beating a staccato rhythm on the lobby's marble floor. Where was that photographer? She was supposed to meet Glynna twenty minutes ago.

Grumbling to herself, she pulled out her cell phone and punched in Missy Thorpe's number. After three rings, voice mail clicked on and a gratingly cheerful voice announced, "Hi, this is Missy Thorpe. I can't take your call right now because I'm out on a photo shoot. But leave your name and number and I'll catch you later!"

Glynna clicked off without leaving a message. Honestly, the girl sounded about sixteen. What had Stacy been thinking? She checked her watch again. Jake would never have been late like this.

She felt a stab of pain at the thought of Jake. She told herself she ought to be happy he was going to New York. After all, he was her friend, and she should be celebrating that he was going to do what he'd always wanted.

But all *she* wanted was for him to stay here with her. She pinched the bridge of her nose, squeezing back tears. What an idiot she'd been—telling him she understood, that she didn't have any claims on him.

Ha! She could pretend to be this sophisticated, woman of the world, ready for a relationship for the sake of great sex only, but all he had to do was walk into a room and her body proved her a liar. She'd fallen for Jake with everything she had and there wasn't a damn thing she could do about it.

The door from the street burst open and a tall, leggy blonde dressed in jeans and a belly-baring top rushed in, almost colliding with a pair of businessmen. The men blushed and stammered in the face of her dazzling smile and backed away, turning to stare at her as she headed toward Glynna. "Sorry I'm late," the woman said. She stuck out her hand. "I'm Missy."

"Hi, Missy." Glynna gave the hand a quick shake, then hitched her messenger bag higher on her shoulders and turned toward the elevators. "We'd better get started. We have a lot of ground to cover."

"Sure thing." Missy followed Glynna to the elevators. "So what exactly is our angle here?"

Glynna punched the down button. "The story's a look at the underground tunnels as a city within a city. A world under our feet that a lot of people still don't know about."

"Nick said it was sort of like the ship channel piece you did. With lots of sex and stuff." She fiddled with something in her camera bag.

Glynna flushed. "Not just sex. Whatever is...unexpected."

"That's cool." The elevator arrived and they stepped on. Missy grinned at Glynna. "So what's it like to work with Jake Dawson?"

She hesitated. *He's amazing* probably wasn't the answer Missy was looking for. "Jake is a very talented photographer," she said.

"He's pretty talented in a lot of ways, I hear." Missy nudged Glynna, almost knocking her off balance. "The man is a real hottie!"

She felt her face burn. "He is, uh, quite good looking."

"He's a total babe." The doors opened and they stepped off. "I sure wouldn't kick him out of my bed."

I didn't kick him out of mine, Glynna thought. *But he left anyway.*

She stopped to consult her map of the tunnel system. "This section is known for whimsical modern art, which should make some good illustrations. We'll want to stop by Beck's Prime, a restaurant with a sidewalk café open to the tunnel foot traffic. We're in the South Louisiana Tunnel now. Later we'll head west, into the North Travis Tunnel. There's a lot of art deco architecture over there."

They set out down a broad "street," lined on either side with elegant shops and offices. Glynna noted a beauty shop, dry cleaners, a deli, an optometrist and a dentist, a bakery, two shoe stores and a men's clothing store. A bookstore advertised the latest bestsellers in its windows, while a banner over a travel agency invited passersby to book a cruise vacation. Everything a person could want was available in the tunnels, without the hassles of traffic, parking or inclement weather.

I wonder if Jake knows about all this, she thought. *He would love it.*

"This is awesome!" Missy exclaimed, aiming her camera at a neon mural. "I can't believe Jake passed up the chance to photograph this."

Another stab of pain. Honestly, what was wrong with her? "Jake's very busy right now," she said.

"So what's he up to?" Missy adjusted a dial on her camera.

"I don't know." She moved past the girl, toward a shoe-shine stand. "I'm going to talk to a few people. Catch up when you can."

She didn't want to talk to Missy about Jake. She didn't want to talk about him at all. Discussing him, even thinking about him, hurt too much. The only thing she knew to do was concentrate on this story and forget about him for a while. She'd always been able to lose herself in her work before. With everything else that had gone wrong in her life, work was the one thing she could count on.

While Missy shot rolls of film, Glynna interviewed the shoe-shine man about life in the tunnels. "It's always cool down here," he said. "All the time. Whole thing is air-conditioned. That's why they built the tunnels, you know? So people wouldn't have to go out in the heat in the summer or the rain in the winter."

Sounds like my life, she thought. Safe and comfortable. No risks. Until she'd spent a wonderful, wild weekend with Jake. Even hurting the way she was now, she wouldn't trade that experience for all the comfort and convenience in the world.

After Glynna talked to the ice-cream shop manager, Missy caught up with her. "My gosh, did you know they have a post office down here? And banks?"

"They have everything," Glynna said. She pointed to a boutique with a display of lingerie in the window. "Let's check this out."

Glynna's shoes sank into the plush mauve carpeting of the boutique, and the scent of sage and citrus wafted around her. Mannequins dressed in expensive silk stared blankly at her, while more lingerie was piled on antique tables. She fingered a black satin bustier trimmed in rhinestones. What would Jake think of this…on her?

"Hot stuff." Missy joined her beside the mannequin. "Of course, I'm more into nudity than dressing up, you know?"

Glynna glanced at the photographer's perfectly flat stomach. Uh-huh. If she had a perfect body, she wouldn't need any "dressing up," either.

Missy fingered a lacy thong. "Wonder if Jake goes for this kind of thing?" she asked. "I'd dress up if I thought it would get me anywhere with him."

Glynna grunted and moved on. Missy followed. "I mean, he and I already have a lot in common, since we're both photographers. I could tell him I want to learn from a master. Think he'd go for it? Then once we got together, we could let nature take its course."

One more word about Jake and Glynna was going to slap this chick. She turned on her heel and exited the store.

"Hey, wait for me!" Missy trotted alongside her. "Where are you off to in such a hurry?"

Glynna consulted her map, then took a right turn

down a wide corridor that resembled an outdoor pedestrian mall, complete with potted trees, bright overhead lighting and windows displaying wares from the various shops. Orange signs announced they were now in the North Travis Tunnel, but the switch to a different section of the system was also signaled by a change in architecture. Here, the gracefully curved columns and geometric decorations harkened back to the heyday of Art Deco in the twenties. The effect was captivating, so that even Missy forgot about Jake for a moment and concentrated on her work.

"Why is everything so different in this section?" Missy asked.

"Each section of the tunnels is maintained by the buildings above it. It's all private property and the owners decorate their own area distinctively…." Glynna's voice trailed off as her eyes focused on the single black-and-white photograph on display in the front window of a small gallery. A tingle raced up her spine as she stared at the softly lighted shot of a nude woman lounging across a shawl-draped chair.

"What is it?" Missy stopped beside her.

"I…" Glynna shook her head, trying to regain her composure. Ignoring Missy, she headed for the gallery. No way could she pass this up.

Bells chimed as she pushed open the door to the gallery. It was a small space, not more than twelve feet by twelve feet, all of it filled with more black-and-white nudes, the simply matted and framed photos arranged along the walls and on pillars in the center of the shop.

Heart pounding, Glynna stared at the photo she'd

seen the day she'd run into Jake in the hall—the one of his friend's wife. Hot waves of longing washed over her as she stared at the woman's full breasts and smooth thighs. Tears clotted at the back of her throat while moisture pooled between her thighs at the memory of Jake posing her on the bed in their cottage at La Paloma. She could almost feel his hands on her again, hear the rough edge of his voice as he told her she was beautiful, see the desire burning in his eyes. Afterward, they'd made love in the tangled sheets, the camera's single eye staring at them like a voyeur, the white light of the uncovered lamp plunging every hollow and valley of their bodies into deep shadow, every curve and uplift into stark relief.

"I think it's disgusting."

Missy's indignant voice startled her from her reverie. She tore her gaze from the photo and stared at her colleague. "What did you say?"

Missy jerked her head in the direction of the photo. "I said, it's disgusting, exploiting women this way." She looked around the room. "I'll bet the photographer is a man."

The clerk in the corner glared at them. Glynna turned back to the photo and spoke in a low voice. "It's not disgusting. It's beautiful."

"What kind of woman would allow herself to be used this way?" Missy had lowered her voice, but her tone was still strident.

Glynna shook her head. "Maybe a woman who appreciated art."

Or a woman in love with the artist. Oh, Jake, what

*am I going to do? Making love to you was the best thing
I'd ever done, but maybe the worst, too.*

"THESE NEW PHOTOS are fantastic, Jake. Your best work
yet." Jake watched with a mixture of pride and regret as
Terrence, the gallery owner, unwrapped the framed photos of Glynna. Terrence held up a shot of Glynna reclin-
ing on the bed, arms overhead, eyes closed as if in sleep.
"I think I'll put this one in the front window."

Jake frowned. He had mixed feelings about sharing
these images with the world. He was convinced it was
his best work, but it was also his most personal. He'd
never been involved with one of his models the way he
was involved with Glynna. The thought of some
stranger buying the images to display in his own rooms
made his stomach clench.

He reached out and touched the frame of the photo in
Terrence's hand, almost overcome by the urge to snatch
it back. "You can display these, but they're not for sale."

Terrence raised one eyebrow. "You sure? They'd sell
in a flash."

He shook his head. "These are going into my personal collection."

The gallery owner looked at the photo in his hand
again. "A special lady, huh?" He smiled. "I didn't know
you were such a romantic."

Neither did I.

"Say, there's a couple of customers in the gallery
now." Terrence folded the paper back over the images of
Glynna and sank back in his chair. "Why don't you go
out and introduce yourself? Might help make the sale."

He shoved his hands into the pockets of his jeans. "I don't know, I'm not really comfortable with that sort of thing."

"Come on." Terrence glanced over his shoulder at the two-way mirror behind his desk. "Couple of good-looking chicks. Go turn on the charm. Convince them you're the next Annie Liebowitz."

He shook his head. He couldn't say no to Terrence. Not after the man had given him a chance like this. "All right." He sighed and pushed open the door into the gallery.

His eyes swept the space until he spotted the two women. They were standing before one of his favorite shots, of his buddy's wife, Denise, on a swing, feet pointed in front of her, back arched, long hair trailing almost to the ground. They'd actually taken that one in a park, at night, his buddy keeping watch, Denise's robe in hand, in case someone came along.

The skinny blonde was pouting, apparently not happy about something, a Linhof camera slung over one shoulder. A fellow photographer who didn't like his work?

He couldn't see any more of the other woman than one hip and shoulder as she moved around the pillar. A flicker of recognition stirred. Who was she?

He started toward the pair, reaching the pillar at the same time the second woman emerged from behind it. His heart stopped beating and his breath caught in his throat. "Glynna!"

Her face blanched white as the marble pillar, then a rosy flush swept over her, like the afterglow of sex. He swallowed, trying to ignore the tightness in his groin. "What are you doing here?" he asked.

Her tongue swept over her lips, a sensuous gesture that made him curl his fingers into fists to keep from reaching for her. "I'm working on the story about the tunnel system." She glanced around the room. "I didn't know this was where your exhibit was. It's…stunning."

She was stunning. He couldn't stop staring at her. The whole point of breaking it off with her had been to allow him to concentrate on his work, but the idea had been a flop. The minute he'd told himself he couldn't have her, he'd wanted her all the more.

"You look great," he said, letting his gaze drop to take in the pink silk shirtdress that flowed over her curves, ending at midthigh. Sheer hose and delicate sling-back sandals made her legs look sexy as hell. He shifted his stance, trying to hide his growing arousal. So much for playing it cool.

"Aren't you going to introduce me?" The blonde inserted herself between them and smiled up at him, eyes bright.

Glynna quickly masked a frown. "This is Missy Thorpe." She gestured to the blonde. "Missy, Jake Dawson."

"I'm so excited to meet you." Missy grabbed his hand and held on, continuing to stare into his eyes. "I'm a big fan of your work." Her smile broadened. "I'm a photographer, too."

He nodded. "I noticed the camera." He looked past her to Glynna. "So, how's it going?"

She nodded. "Okay. The tunnels are really interesting."

"Yeah." He felt like an idiot, but he couldn't keep from staring at her.

"I'm the photographer for this feature." Missy claimed his attention once more. She was still clinging to his hand. He tried to pull away, but she held on. "We could have lunch. You could give me some pointers."

"Maybe some other time." His eyes met Glynna's again. She seemed to be fighting back laughter. "Uh, Glynna, can I talk to you a minute? Alone?"

Missy frowned, but he was finally able to extricate himself from her grip. He nodded to her, then took Glynna's arm and steered her toward the corner. "What's so funny?" he asked her.

"You should have seen the look on your face when she latched on to you. And the look on *her* face!" She chuckled. "Missy has a huge crush on you. You're all she's talked about this morning."

He glanced back at the blonde. She smiled and waved. He frowned and turned back to Glynna. "Not my type."

"Are you sure?" Her tone was teasing, her eyes shining with mirth. "She says she wouldn't kick you out of her bed."

"I prefer curvy brunettes." He let his hand drift to her waist, breaking his own rule about staying away from her. He usually had great willpower, but then, everything was different with Glynna.

"Hmm. I'll confess I'd much rather be working with you." She glanced back toward Missy. "She's driving me crazy."

Reluctantly, he took his hand away. "Then ditch her."

"How?"

He thought a minute. "How about if I distract her? You leave the gallery. Walk around the corner and you'll see a service elevator. Take it up one floor to the parking level and wait for me there."

"What if she follows?"

"I'll tell her you headed in the other direction."

She nodded. "Then what?"

"Then I'll take you to lunch." He had so much he wanted to tell her—about the freelance work he'd found to carry him over the first few weeks in New York, and the subletter he'd found for his condo. As much as anything, he'd missed talking to her.

She hesitated, then nodded. "All right."

She left him and said something to Missy, then headed out the door. He walked over to the photographer. "So what do you think of my work?" He indicated the photos. It was a dangerous question, one he ordinarily never asked. What artist wanted to risk criticism?

Her mouth dropped open. "They're yours?" Two bright spots of red formed on her cheeks. "I…I had no idea!"

"Yes." He traced one finger along the frame of Denise's photo. "What do you think?"

She stiffened. "They're, uh, very interesting. But, um, why nude women?"

He smiled. "I like women."

Missy's frown deepened. "Don't you feel that photographing women nude, in these helpless and subjective postures, is demeaning and chauvinistic?"

He stared at her. Had she read this diatribe somewhere, or did she really believe it? "No."

"But don't you think…"

He stopped listening. A glance toward the door told him Glynna was safely out of sight. He checked his watch, then looked at Missy, who was gathering steam, spouting off something about "voyeurism" and "sexual oppression." "Listen, this is fascinating, but I have to go. Maybe we'll finish this conversation some other time."

She gaped at him and he took advantage of her silence to make for the door. He stopped before exiting to look back at her. She was turning in a circle, eyes searching the small space. "If you're looking for Glynna, I think she headed back toward the Bank One building," he said.

He didn't wait for an answer, but ducked out the door and down the corridor. One flight up, Glynna was waiting for him.

14

GLYNNA WAITED outside the service elevator for Jake to meet her. The sensible part of her said she ought to turn around and run as fast as she could away from him, to keep her heart from being hurt further. But that advice was drowned out by the need to be with him again. If she could only talk to him, see him, touch him, maybe it would be enough to ease his parting. He was going away, but he wasn't gone yet. Why not make the most of what time they had and grieve later, when she was alone?

The elevator doors slid open and he stepped out. She took a deep breath, trying to remain calm, unaffected. "Did you manage to avoid Missy?" she asked, watching him out of the corner of her eye.

"She's gone." He took her hand and pulled her into the elevator. The door closed behind them and the car started up.

"Where should we have lunch?" she asked. She could smell the herbal shampoo he used, and the faint astringent odor of photo chemicals. The familiar scents made her nerves hum with awareness.

He shoved his hands in his pockets and avoided looking at her. "What do you feel like having?"

She shifted from one foot to the other. She wasn't hungry, at least not for food. "I don't know. What are you in the mood for?"

He leaned forward and punched the stop button. The elevator lurched to a halt. She staggered, and stared at him. Before she could speak, he pulled her into his arms. "I'm in the mood for this," he whispered, and covered her mouth with his own.

It was a deep, drowning kiss, the kind that swept away all awareness of everything else but his warm lips pressed against hers, his tongue teasing her, his arms holding her so tightly against him. He cradled her head in his hand, the other at her back as he feathered kisses along her jaw. Desire rose in her, filling her with delicious heat and tension, overwhelming caution and inhibition.

She slid her hands down his back, pulling him closer still, pressing to him, relishing the feel of his arousal, hard and hot against her stomach. "I've missed you," she said.

"I've missed you, too." His mouth moved lower, painting a row of gentle, suctioning kisses down her throat and along the neckline of her dress. "I tried to stay away, but then I saw you today and all I could think of was how you'd looked when I'd photographed you. Naked." He reached up and began to unbutton her dress. "I want to see you that way again."

As his mouth followed his fingers down the front of her dress and cool air rushed across her feverish skin, some semblance of propriety asserted itself. "What if someone tries to use the elevator?" she asked.

"They won't." His voice vibrated against her stomach, sending tremors through her. "It's a freight elevator, one that isn't used much. If they see it stopped, they'll assume someone's unloading something or that it's out of service. There's another elevator around the corner they can use."

"Oh." She couldn't manage any more. He'd unfastened the clasp of her bra and pushed it aside and now he was kissing his way across her breasts.

"The person who invented bras that open in the front should get a medal," he said.

"Yesssss." Whether she was agreeing with him or exulting over the sensation of his mouth on her, she couldn't have said. As his tongue swept over her nipple, her vision lost focus. She closed her eyes and sagged against the quilted covering on the elevator walls.

He transferred his attention to her other breast, each movement of his mouth sending new waves of arousal through her, until she was literally shaking with need.

Keeping a steady hand at her waist, he rose to his full height and looked her in the eye. "Have you ever made love standing up before?" he asked.

She swallowed, "No. Have you?"

He smiled and brushed her hair away from her face. "Not with you. And not in an elevator." He looked around. "But the padded walls are nice."

He reached down and undid the button at her waist, but she grabbed his wrist to stop him. "Wait a minute. It's my turn."

He gave her a questioning look, but withdrew his hand and waited. She reached up and undid the top button of his shirt, forcing herself to move slowly, to draw out the exquisite excitement of the moment.

When she shoved the shirt back over his shoulders, he unfastened the cuffs and removed the garment altogether, then drew her to him. She sighed as her damp, aching nipples brushed against the soft hair on his chest. He held her a moment, kissing her shoulder, letting the tension subside a little, before he moved to her buttons once more.

The last button parted and he pushed the two halves of the dress aside and ran his thumb under the waistband of her panty hose. "You're not wearing any underwear," he said.

She grinned. "That's why they're called panty hose."

"Hmm." He dragged his thumb along the center seam, down to the thin cotton crotch. She sucked in her breath as he stroked her through the fabric. "You're soaking wet," he murmured.

All she could manage was a whimper as he dropped to his knees and began to kiss her. She braced her hands on his shoulders, her muscles tightening with each tantalizing stroke.

He paused and looked up at her. "How much do you care about these hose?"

She blinked. "What do you mean?"

"Would you be upset if I ripped them?"

Heat lanced through her at the thought. She shook her head.

He hooked his finger around the seam and tugged, tearing the nylon, then using both hands to widen the opening until she was exposed. As his tongue swept over her, her knees buckled, but he held her up, pushing her back against the wall.

She gripped his shoulders, the muscles of her thighs straining as he teased and suckled, until she was incoherent with wanting. It was too much, really, all her senses on hyperalert, the strange posture and the unfamiliar location adding to her distraction. She pushed on his shoulder. "Wait. Stop."

He withdrew, resting his head on her thigh and cradling her. "What is it?" he asked. "What's wrong?"

"I want you up here with me," she said.

He rose, smiling, and she reached for the top button of his pants. He started to pull her close, then stilled, his smile vanished. He groaned and beat his head against the padding.

"What is it?" she asked, alarmed.

His forehead still resting against the wall, he gave her a sheepish smile. "I didn't exactly plan this, you know."

"What do you mean?" She frowned.

He straightened and shook his head. "No condoms."

Relief made her sag against the side of the elevator. She smiled. "Hand me my purse."

She found the condom in the zippered inner pocket, where she'd put it days ago, in case of an "emergency." Surely this qualified.

Desire built within her once more when he unfastened his jeans and freed his erection. He held out his hand for the condom, but she shook her head. "Oh, no. The pleasure is all mine."

She heard the sharp intake of his breath at her touch, and a thrill rushed through her. How many women shared Missy's opinion that Jake was a man they "wouldn't kick out of bed"? But *she* was the one he wanted to be with.

He was heavy in her hand, hot and hard and when she bent to sheath him the memory of him filling her made her tremble. She raised her eyes to meet his and the strength of his gaze reached inside of her, beyond mere lust to something much deeper. Was it possible that Jake's feelings for her went further than friendship? Was the intensity of their coming together due to more than physical compatibility?

Her eyes stung with tears at the thought, but before she could speak, he had gently pushed her away. "Spread your legs wide," he said, his voice low and gruff.

She did as he asked, and felt him enter her, her muscles contracting around him, her heart leaping with joy at the sensation. She stood on tiptoe and clutched at his shoulders, breathing in ragged gasps.

His hands slipped beneath her bottom, lifting her. "Wrap your legs around my waist," he ordered.

She did so, locking her ankles together. He braced her back against the wall and began to thrust, hard and deep, each movement shuddering through her, sending her spiraling upward once more.

She clung to him, surrendering to the onslaught, dimly aware of the heavy rasp of his breathing, the slickness of sweat on his back and shoulders, the muscles of his thighs knotting against her own taut flesh. There was something elemental about this mating, something wild and animal and more erotic than anything they had done before. Yet, cradled in his arms, supported wholly by him, she felt an overwhelming tenderness, a caring that made tears prick her eyes and her heart clench.

She tried to stifle a scream as her climax ripped through her, but her cries echoed off the padded walls, followed closely by his own shout of triumph. His final thrusts made the elevator rock and sent her back scraping against the padding. And then they were still, her arms wrapped around his head, cradling him to her shoulder.

Gradually, he let her unwind her legs from his waist and slide to the floor. He leaned against her, only his propped arms saving her from being crushed. He kissed her cheek, then her mouth, and smiled. "Have I told you lately that you're amazing?"

She kissed him long and hard in answer. She didn't trust herself to speak yet. What they'd shared just now seemed beyond words.

They dressed quickly, then he started the elevator again. They emerged in a hallway off the bank lobby, two ordinarily dressed people, though Glynna wondered if they didn't look a bit disheveled.

He took her arm and guided her toward the front doors. "What say we have that lunch now?"

They found a small Mexican restaurant a few blocks away and ordered iced tea and fajitas. He settled back in the booth across from her. "Other than the annoying Missy, how is the story on the tunnels going?" he asked.

"Fine. There's a lot of material there. Great history. Interesting places." She squeezed lemon into her tea and eyed him over her glass. "What brought you to the gallery today? Do you visit often to see how things are going?"

He shook his head. "I was delivering some new

photos." He tore open a paper packet of sugar and dumped it into his glass. "The ones I took of you."

The lemon wedge fell from her hand and slid across the table. She stared at him. "You're putting my photos on display?"

"They're my best work." He smiled. "The owner, Terrence, was stunned when I showed them to him."

She folded her hands in her lap to hide their trembling. "How could you do that?"

He frowned. "How could I not? Did you expect me to keep those gorgeous pictures to myself?"

She looked away, stung by his answer. "Yes, I did. I posed for you. Not for every stranger who walks by."

He leaned toward her. "The photos *are* special to me. But I want everyone to see how special." When she continued to ignore him, he drew back again. "I thought you liked my work. You said it was sensitive and artistic."

She took a long swig of tea, struggling to remain calm. "Your photos of other women are art—mine is different." She forced herself to look at him, to not flinch at the confusion in his eyes. How could he not understand? "You have to take the photos of me out of your show."

"No." His expression softened a little. "Look, if you're worried about someone recognizing you, they won't. Your face is hidden, and no one expects to see you like that."

No one expects cold Ms. McCormick to pose nude for her lover. The thought hurt almost as much as his betrayal. "This isn't about me," she said. "I trusted you and you abused that trust."

"I'm a photographer. It's what I do. When I asked

you to pose for me, I assumed you knew I would use the photos as I saw fit."

"I posed for *you*." She spoke around a knot of tears. "As a gift for you. Not so you could...could *use* me." It was bad enough that he was going away, but she'd comforted herself with the knowledge that at least she'd have the memory of the time they'd shared to soothe her. For him to take one of those memories and...exploit it... It was too much to bear. She threw her napkin on the table and stood. "If you don't understand the difference, there's no sense talking to you anymore."

He reached for her, but she ducked away, moving blindly for the door. She had to get out of here, away from him before she burst out crying and made more of a fool of herself than she already had.

NICK GLANCED over his shoulder to make sure the coast was clear, then slipped into Stacy's empty office. He'd seen her leave for lunch ten minutes ago and figured he had a good half hour before she was likely to return.

He went straight to her desk and began searching the drawers. He didn't know what he expected to find—anything that would give him an upper hand in this game they were playing. She'd challenged him to figure out what she wanted from him. If that meant tossing her office behind her back, well, who had said he had to play fair?

He frowned at the orderly rows of hanging files, the neatly arranged office supplies and stacks of stationery. Couldn't she have a diary stashed here somewhere? Something that would give him a glimpse into her fantasies and desires?

He opened the bottom drawer and sorted through the spare packet of stockings, protein bars, bottled water, hair spray and a makeup kit. He looked at the stockings again. Stockings, not panty hose. Now there was a clue, though he wasn't sure what he could do with it. He was about to close the drawer when a book at the bottom caught his eye.

He pulled out the paperback. It had a pink and purple cover, with the title *Ransomed Bride* in gold script across the cover. A muscular, bare-chested man clutched a bosomy blonde close to him in the cover illustration. Nick grinned and flipped through the book.

So Stacy was a closet romance reader? He'd pictured her as a literature snob. He skimmed the text. This passage was a battle scene—a Viking raid on some village. Exciting stuff.

A noise in the hall made him shove the book back in the desk and close the drawer. When Stacy walked in, he was standing by the window, as if he'd been enjoying the view.

"Nick. What are you doing here?"

He turned and smiled. "Hello, Stacy. Have you seen the article in *The Chronicle?*"

"About *Texas Style?*" She smiled. "Yes, I have." She pulled a copy from under her arm. "'New editor Stacy Southern has worked a miracle makeover at the stodgy biweekly, taking it from halting to hip, from stale to sexy,'" she read.

He leaned over her shoulder, the herbal smell of her hair making his pulse race. "Don't forget the 'cutting-edge art direction of Nick Castillo has made the magazine as visually pleasing as it is editorially compelling.'"

She laughed. "All right, you get some credit, too."

"Has Gordon seen this yet?"

She shook her head. "At least I haven't shown it to him. Even *he* can't complain about this."

He settled one hip on the corner of her desk. "Why don't we have dinner tonight to celebrate?"

She gave him a speculative look. "Just dinner?"

"We'll start with dinner." With any luck, they'd end up at his place for dessert.

She shook her head. "I don't know…."

"What will you do otherwise—have a glass of champagne alone at your apartment?" Her hurt look told him the remark had hit a bull's-eye. He softened his tone. "I have reservations at Realto." The trendy new restaurant was a gourmet hot spot.

She nodded. "All right. We can meet at the restaurant."

He stood. "I'll pick you up. Six-thirty."

"Do you know where I live?"

"I looked it up in the company directory." He grinned. "I've been doing my homework. I'm learning all sorts of interesting things about you."

OVER OYSTERS ROCKEFELLER and strip steaks, Nick told Stacy about Jake's idea for the photo-essay. "He wants to focus on public art, but on the ways in which people use it—for shade, for shelter or sanctuary. So you'd have all kinds of different people doing things with the backdrop of the art."

She toyed with her empty wineglass and nodded. "I like it. I don't know when we'll run it, but I'll find a place."

She slid her fingers up and down the slender stem of the glass, the unconscious gesture sending his libido into overdrive. Arousal had hummed between them all evening. One look in her eyes and he knew she felt it, too.

When the check came, he reached for it, but she insisted they split the bill. He let her win the argument, waited until they were alone again, then reached across the table and took her hand.

"So where are we going with this, Stace?" He rubbed his thumb against her palm, refusing to let her pull away. "You know you're hot for me and you definitely make me hot. Why are we still tiptoeing around each other this way?"

"You're used to getting every woman you want, aren't you?"

"And women get what they want from me." He kissed her wrist, pressing his tongue against her rapidly beating pulse. "I'm good in bed, and that's not bragging."

She watched him through half-closed eyes, her breathing shallow. "I want a little more than that, Nick."

"What do you want then?"

"That's for you to figure out."

"You want me to read your mind?"

"You need to use your mind, to figure out what turns me on. It shouldn't be that difficult."

He sat back, studying her. She was wearing the same gray, tailored suit and a white silk blouse with pearl buttons she'd had on at the office. She was the picture of the hard-as-nails, take-charge woman. "I know you enjoy words. I'll bet you like to talk during sex. You get off on someone telling you what they're going to do to you, how they're going to make you feel."

. A half smile softened her expression. "You're getting the right idea. What else?"

He let his gaze drop to the neckline of her blouse, to the barely visible cleft between her breasts. Was she wearing something soft and lacy beneath the sharply tailored suit? Was her no-nonsense exterior a front for someone much more…vulnerable? He thought of the romance novel he'd found in her desk. The one with the Viking on the cover. Could it be that Stacy's secret fantasy was to be swept away by a dashing he-man? To be the one who wasn't in charge for a change?

He looked at her a moment longer, then made his decision, Standing, he pulled her from her chair. "Come on. Let's go back to my place."

She stared at him. "I don't think so."

He slid his hands down her arms to her wrists, capturing and holding her, then leaned his body into hers. "I think so. I know what you want and I intend to give it to you." He kissed her, his lips hard against hers, his tongue sweeping into her mouth, staking a claim. No more playing the tentative gentleman, trying to guess how she wanted him to behave. Time to let instinct take over.

When he raised his head, she stared at him, dazed. "Nick, I…"

"Come on, let's go." Still holding her wrists, he pulled her along, to the elevators leading to the parking garage. He stood behind her, his body pressed to hers, so she'd have no doubt about how much he wanted her. While the lighted numbers ticked off their descent, he let go of her wrists and slid his hands u₋ breasts. "What are you wearing under this b. whispered into her ear.

"Wouldn't you like to know?" Her words held some of her old bravado, but the tremble in her voice gave her away.

He traced his thumbs along her ribcage, rubbing against the band of her bra. "Take it off."

She tried to pull away from him. "No!"

He held her close and traced his tongue around the shell of her ear. "Take it off and give it to me."

For a half a beat, he thought she'd refuse again. Then she slipped out of her suit jacket and handed it to him. Then she reached into her blouse and undid the clasp of her bra. Pulling her arms free of the straps, she slid the scrap of lingerie out one sleeve and held it up.

The bra was made of white lace, sexy and feminine and still warm from her skin. He folded his fingers around it and shoved it in his jacket pocket. In the glare of the florescent lighting he could see the shadow of her nipples beneath the silk of her blouse, erect tips pressed against the fabric. He swallowed hard and took a deep breath, trying to keep in control.

He avoided touching her until they reached the car. He stopped her as she started to climb into the passenger seat, and slid his hand beneath her skirt. Just as he'd hoped, she was wearing stockings and garters, and silky bikinis. "Take these off, too," he said, sliding one finger under the waistband of her panties.

She shook her head and opened her mouth to protest, but his finger slid lower, into the crisp curls, parting her damp folds. "Take them off," he said, stopping himself from moving any farther. "I want to think about you naked under your clothes on the drive home."

The silk was damp, smelling of her musk. His erection forced itself painfully against his fly as he slid into the driver's seat and started the car. He hoped the drive to his apartment would give him time to cool off a little.

He headed out onto the freeway, the air conditioner blast easing his fever some, soothing music on the radio calming his jangled nerves. He tried not to think about the woman beside him. Not yet. He didn't want things to be over with too soon.

He flipped the signal for his exit and turned his head to make sure the lane beside him was clear. A movement out of the corner of his eye distracted him, and he did glance at Stacy then.

Big mistake. She was watching him, a half smile on her lips as she flicked one red-tipped nail over her silk-covered nipple.

He stifled a groan and jerked his attention back to the road, gripping the steering wheel until his knuckles ached. She leaned toward him. "But I thought you liked *visual* stimulus," she cooed.

He said nothing, just kept his eyes forward and drove. But that only gave his imagination more room to run wild.

When they reached his apartment, he handed her the keys. "It's number 3G. Let yourself in, take off all your clothes and go into the bedroom."

She frowned at him. "What if I don't want to?"

The look he gave her was full of desire. "I know you

want to." He leaned toward her. "You're always in charge, aren't you? Making the decisions, running the show. You have to be. It's how you've gotten where you are. But tonight, I'll call the shots. All you have to do is follow instructions…and enjoy." He traced one finger along her jaw, coming to rest over her racing pulse.

She wet her lips. "All right."

He watched her walk away, the fabric of her skirt sliding over her hips, the way he wanted to slide his hand over her naked skin. He forced himself to wait five minutes, timing it by his watch, imagining her lying on his bed, naked, impatient for him.

He slipped into his apartment as quietly as possible, stopping in the living room to strip off his clothes before he moved on to the bedroom.

She was stretched out on top of the comforter, her skin like ivory in the glow of the track lighting over the bed. He paused in the doorway to take in the sight of her. When her eyes met his, he let out a deep breath and smiled. "You're beautiful," he said.

"I feel ridiculous." She raised up on her elbows to glare at him.

"You don't look ridiculous." He went to his closet and pulled four ties from the rack on the wall. He'd just thought of this part. She wouldn't like it at first, but he was sure she'd change her mind.

"What are you doing?" she asked when he reached for her wrist and knotted the tie around it.

"I'm making it so you *have* to let me take charge." He wrapped the other end of the tie around the bedpost and tightened it.

"You're crazy," she said, but she didn't resist as he moved to her other wrist.

When she was all tied up, he lay beside her on the bed, and slid his hand over her stomach. "What are you going to do now?" she asked, eyeing him warily.

"I'm going to make love to you." He kissed the corner of her mouth, her chin, her throat, her breastbone. "I'm going to make love to your breasts." He lapped his tongue across her nipple, then drew it into his mouth, letting his teeth drag across it. He did the same to her other breast, licking and suckling until she was writhing beneath him, making breathless, mewling noises that tested his control to the limits.

"I'm going to make love to your whole body," he said, and kissed the ridge of each rib, tasting his way across her stomach, plunging his tongue into the dip of her naval. He raised his head to look at her. She arched against the bed, eyes closed, her features softened by desire. "Do you like that?" he asked.

She nodded. "Yes." Her answer was a breathy whisper. "Don't stop."

"I won't stop." He moved down farther, to the soft thatch, damp with the evidence of her arousal. He slid one finger inside her, and felt her muscles contract around him. He stilled, waiting. Teasing her.

She arched against his hand. "Don't stop," she said again.

He withdrew his hand. "Uh-uh. I'm the one giving orders here. Remember?"

He slid up her body and lay beside her once more, holding her close, letting the tension subside a little. The tenderness he felt as he cradled her caught him off guard. He was Mr. Physical Gratification. In it for the fun. Sex wasn't supposed to be serious.

Except somewhere along the way, things had changed with Stacy. He wanted to make this special for her. To show her he was more than a shallow player, that he wasn't out to hurt her.

He kissed her, a slow, lingering caress at odds with the urgency building within him. While his mouth explored her lips, he smoothed his hands down her body, tracing his fingers across her sensitive breasts, smoothing the satiny skin of her stomach, shaping his palms to her muscular thighs. He cupped her crotch and she arched against him, her need for him making his throat tighten.

She cried out when he left her, but he kissed her forehead and stroked her cheek. "I'm just going to get a condom."

The box was in his bedside table. He tore open the foil packet and sheathed himself, slowly, watching her watching him as he did so. Her eyes were dark with passion, her breathing shallow, the naked longing on her face so unlike the tough mask she usually wore.

He knelt between her legs where she was opened to him. He entered slowly, letting her take her fill of him. His vision clouded as she squeezed around him, and he groaned. He reached down and parted her folds until he found the bud of her clit, his hand moving in time with his strokes, slowly at first, then more swiftly.

She came quickly, the exquisite tension and release driving his own need. As her cries echoed in the stillness, he reached up and loosened her hands. She slid her arms around him, holding him close, with a tenderness that was his final undoing. He screamed her name as he came, driving into her, aftershocks rocking them both, until they collapsed together, sated, still holding each other close, as if they'd never let go.

15

THE PROBLEM with running away from your problems was that you could only go so far, Glynna thought as she stared glumly at the blank screen of her computer. When she'd fled from the restaurant and Jake last week, she hadn't been running away from him so much as she'd been trying to escape her own confused feelings. Yes, she'd been hurt that he considered his photo of her more art than memento, but when she was alone and being brutally honest with herself, she had to admit he'd never misled her.

She'd misled herself, falling in love with a man who'd made it clear he put his career first. Jake was physically attracted to her; maybe he even felt something deeper, but it wasn't enough to change his mind about leaving.

Fine. She straightened and clicked on the pull-down menu of her word-processing program. Jake wasn't the only one who could put his career first. She knew for a fact that "Underground Houston," the piece she'd turned in, was one of the best things she'd ever written. She'd be surprised if it didn't win an award. Even her father wouldn't be able to ignore that. And not being with

Jake would give her more time to work on other things. For instance, she had a great idea for a story on the plight of Vietnamese fishermen working along the Gulf Coast. Or she might do a piece on underage strippers...

The intercom buzzed, making her jump, and her father's voice barked over the speaker. "Glynna, I want to see you in my office immediately."

She sighed and leaned over to depress the answer button. "I'll be right there." What crisis would he demand she take care of at once? What mess would he expect her to untangle?

She paused at her office door to take a deep breath. This time, she'd find the courage to stand up to him. She'd explain that she couldn't drop everything to handle his problems. He wouldn't ask it of any other employee, so he shouldn't ask it of her. Gordon was a reasonable man. He'd respect her for standing up for herself.

Shaky confidence somewhat bolstered, she headed down the hall for the publisher's office.

"Come in," he barked at her knock.

"You wanted to see me?" She stood in front of his desk, trying not to look like a guilty schoolgirl. When he didn't ask her to sit down, she sat anyway. At least from this angle, she could look him in the eye.

The gaze that met hers was anything but warm. He shoved a stack of papers toward her. "What is the meaning of this?"

She recognized the galleys of her piece on the tunnel system. The one she'd been so proud of. She cleared her throat. "It's the feature I wrote on the downtown tunnels." She forced herself to keep her chin up, her expression unemotional. "I thought it turned out very well."

"Oh, you did, did you?" He picked up the galleys and scanned the first page, then began to read, "Step from the elevator into the downtown tunnels and you enter a secret part of the city. A place of wide avenues lined with sidewalk cafés and trendy boutiques, where the lilt of soft music and conversation replace the roar of traffic, and lush tropical trees and overflowing flower boxes lend an air of elegance and romance."

She'd been particularly proud of that opening. It set the right tone for her story. She wasn't writing an inventory of shops and businesses; she wanted to transport her readers to another time and place, to capture their imaginations and entertain them.

Her father's voice droned on. "In this place originally designed for the convenience of businessmen, it's easy to imagine the setting for a tryst: lovers meeting to share drinks and heated glances at a small bistro, then walking hand in hand past elegant Art Deco columns and flickering neon. They pause to admire a display of expensive lingerie in the window of a boutique. Perhaps he buys her a special bit of lace and satin to wear later. They move on, to a showing of artistic nudes in a fine art gallery, stopping to embrace in a shadowed nook. Only a short elevator ride will take them up to their plush hotel room, where fantasies begun in the other world of the tunnels will come to life."

She flushed, remembering her own tryst in the tunnels. She and Jake hadn't waited for a hotel room. Their need for each other had been so intense. So urgent…

The sharp slap of the papers on the desk made her jump. "What kind of journalism is this? It reads like some torrid romance novel."

She dug her fingernails into her palm and swallowed angry words. She was determined to remain reasonable, even if her father did not. "I was setting a mood, taking our readers on an adventure. They can find facts and figures in chamber of commerce brochures. We want to give them something more. Something…artistic."

"Hogwash! No one will take us seriously if we print blather like this. The papers are already comparing us to some sex rag."

"I believe *The Chronicle* said we were 'sexy, edgy and daring.' I understand we've gained new advertisers and new readers."

"We've also lost readers and advertisers. People and companies who have been with us for twenty years." Something besides anger tinged his voice. Regret? As if a veil had been pulled aside, she suddenly saw how tired her father looked. How old. Maybe all these changes were too much for him. Too sudden.

She leaned toward him, her voice gentle. "We're growing and changing. Is that so bad?"

"It's bad when some reporter refers to my daughter as 'a writer with an erotic flair' and 'a woman who knows her way around a sexy double entendre.'" He scowled at her, deep lines etched around his eyes and mouth. "Is that the kind of reputation you want?"

She colored. After being a nondescript nobody for so long, was having someone see her as sexy and erotic—

even if only on paper—such a bad thing? "I think you're overreacting," she said.

"Oh, you do?" He planted both hands flat on the desk and leaned toward her. "You're still my daughter. *And* my employee. And until I say different, you will no longer be writing features for this magazine."

She swayed, suddenly dizzy. "Wh…what are you saying?"

"I'm saying I'm sure we can find some back of the book pieces for you to work on that won't damage your reputation any further. And you can continue your work as my assistant, of course."

Of course. Frustration blocked her throat, and hot tears threatened at the back of her eyes. If she had any courage, she'd tell him she quit. She'd go somewhere else. Find a job where she was appreciated.

"I'm sorry to have to do this, but I expected better of you, Glynna. But I'm giving you a second chance, something I wouldn't do for just anyone."

The disappointment in his eyes made her feel ten years old again. She'd cheated on a math test, hoping to please him with an A. Instead, she'd been caught and punished. But the worst punishment was knowing she'd failed him. She always let him down.

"You may go now." He turned his back and she bolted for the door. She had to get out of here before she disgraced herself further with tears. Tears of anger and shame. Anger that he had such little faith in her. Shame that she couldn't find it in herself to stand up to him. She'd never win his respect—his love. So why did she keep trying?

JAKE GUIDED the motorcycle into an empty space in the parking garage, cut the engine and whipped off his helmet. He slung his saddlebag over his shoulder and headed toward the elevator, boot heels echoing on the concrete. He wouldn't make many more visits like this to the *Texas Style* offices. He'd planned on turning in his resignation a week ago, but things kept getting in the way. Like the photo-essay Nick had asked for, and other loose ends he had to tie up. But he'd cut ties with the magazine soon, and then he'd be free to go to New York and start making things happen.

An unfamiliar noise intruded on his thoughts as he neared the elevator. He stopped, listening, and was sure he heard crying. He glanced around the garage. It seemed deserted, but there was definitely someone down here. A child or a woman, hurt or in pain.

He started walking toward the sound, his steps coming faster as he recognized Glynna's car, with Glynna slumped in the front seat, the windows rolled down, the engine off. He began to run, heart hammering. Had someone attacked her? Was she hurt?

She glanced up and saw him, and hastily scrubbed at her face with a wadded handkerchief. By the time he reached her, she was eyeing him warily. "Hello, Jake."

"Glynna, what's wrong? Are you all right?"

"I'm fine." She sniffed and stared out the front windshield.

He leaned down, his head in the open window. "You don't look all right." He traced the tear tracks on her cheek. "Why are you crying?"

She turned away, but not before he saw the pain in her eyes. "What's made you so sad?" he asked.

"I'm not sad. I'm furious!" She hit her hand against the steering wheel and he pulled back.

"If this is about the photos I took of you—"

"Everything is not about you, you know!"

Her words were like a slap in the face. His cheeks burned. "Okay. I guess I deserved that." He crouched down beside the car, his face more or less level with hers. "So who are you angry with?"

"My father. Gordon 'Mr. Self-Righteous' McCormick!" She glared at him. "He pulled my piece on the tunnel system and until *he* decides differently, I'm no longer a feature writer."

What a bastard. "Why did he do that?"

"Because he wouldn't know fun and sexy if it climbed up on the conference table and did a dance!" She burst into tears again and covered her face with her hands.

To think Jake had once said those words about Glynna. He'd been so wrong. He awkwardly patted her shoulder, wishing she'd get out of the car so he could really hold her. But maybe that wasn't such a good idea. He wanted them to part as friends, not quarreling lovers. "Tell me about the story," he said when her tears had subsided. "What do *you* think of it?"

"I think it's one of the best things I've ever written. It's creative and evocative and entertaining. Not boring or ordinary, which is all he wants."

"Then screw him."

At her startled look, he grinned. "Send the piece to someone else. Someone who'll appreciate it." His grin broadened. "Send it to *Upscale Houston*."

Her eyes widened more. *Upscale Houston* was *Texas Style*'s chief competitor. "I can't do that."

"Why not? Gordon had his chance and turned it down. If you have faith in the piece, why stuff it in a drawer? You don't have a contract that says you can't do freelance work, do you?"

She shook her head. "No. I never thought of it before."

He squeezed her shoulder. "Do it. I bet they'll love it."

She hesitated, then nodded. "Okay. I will." She smiled. "Thanks."

He straightened. "I'm glad I got the chance to see you again."

She smoothed the wet handkerchief in her lap. "I shouldn't have run out of the restaurant the other day." Her eyes met his, red-rimmed and sad. "I owe you an apology. You never misled me about those photos. I just…assumed things I shouldn't have."

"Listen, I—"

She shook her head. "No, let's leave it at that." She turned the key and the car's engine roared to life. "When are you leaving for New York?"

"Soon. I still have some things I need to do." He still had to let his subletter know when he could move in, and he'd put off making plane reservations so long he'd probably have to pay some ridiculous full-priced fare. And there was the matter of his resignation….

"Maybe I'll see you again before you go," she said.

"You bet." He wouldn't leave without saying goodbye, though maybe that's what he'd really been putting off.

Before he could say anything else, she backed out of the parking space. "Wait!" he shouted, but she either didn't hear him, or pretended not to. He watched as she drove away, a tightness in his chest like a hand squeezing his heart. He hadn't had a chance to explain about the photos. To make her understand how special she truly was to him.

UPSTAIRS, Jake delivered the photo-essay to Nick. The art director studied the images of homeless people, children and lunching businessmen against backdrops of urban art around the city. "Terrific stuff," he said. "I wish you were sticking around to do more of this for us."

"I'm amazed you were able to get Stacy to agree to even one photo-essay like this. She always wanted more space for editorial and less for art."

"Oh, Stacy and I have an...understanding." He picked up what looked like a small blue stone from the desk blotter and turned it over and over in his hand. On closer inspection, Jake realized it was a button from a woman's jacket. Stacy's jacket? Exactly what kind of *understanding* did the two have?

When Nick looked up, Jake masked his curiosity. "I hear Gordon pulled the tunnels piece."

Nick made a face. "Yeah. We're going to run this in its place."

"What does Stacy say?"

"She was ready to turn in her resignation, but I persuaded her it would be better to confront Gordon head-on. They had it out and he agreed to give the piece another try later, as long as Glynna doesn't write it."

"That's bullshit." Anger tasted bitter in his throat. "She's the best writer he's got."

"Yeah, but she's also his daughter." Nick shrugged. "I think he's having a hard time thinking of his little girl and sex in the same sentence."

"She's a grown woman. He needs to get over it."

Nick chuckled. "I gotta admit, she never struck me as hot before, but you read her writing now…" He gave Jake a speculative look. "You wouldn't have anything to do with that, would you?"

"What do you mean?"

"I don't know. I got the impression you and Glynna might have had something going on."

Jake looked away. "*Had* being the key word there."

"What happened?"

"Nothing happened." He picked up his saddlebag. "I'm going to New York. She's staying here. We both agreed it was time to end it. We're still friends."

"Right. I always get that defensive talking about my friends."

"Stuff it, Nick."

"Yeah, yeah. So how much longer do we have you with us? A few more issues, I hope."

He shook his head. "I don't think so. My friend was expecting me in New York last week, but I got tied up here. I really need to finish up and get going."

"Don't be in a hurry to clean out your desk. Like I said before, wish we could find a way to make you stay." Nick stuck out his hand. "Good luck in the Big Apple."

They shook hands and Jake headed down the hall, toward the elevators. He passed Glynna's office, and paused to look in. It was empty, of course, the desk as orderly as he remembered it. But the sight of that desk-top kindled other memories—of Glynna stripping for him, teasing him, and of the two of them making love there. She'd surprised him that day, and staked another claim on his heart. He'd never told her how really special she was to him.

He turned away, depression gaining on him like a winter storm. There was a lot he'd regret about his relationship with Glynna, most of all that he had to leave her at all.

16

STACY PAUSED outside Gordon McCormick's office and took a deep breath. Dealing with Gordon was her least favorite part of this job, but she could say he presented a worthwhile challenge. He never treated her like an empty-headed female—just one with a head full of wrong ideas.

Her firm knock was answered by a brusque "Come in."

He looked up from a stack of computer printouts as she approached his desk. "Stacy. What is it?"

She settled into the plush leather chair across from him. "I wanted to talk to you about the next issue. I want to continue the series on special Houston places."

He turned his attention back to the documents. "Yes, yes. We agreed you would choose the editorial content. I've kept my word on that, despite my reservations."

She stiffened, but kept a pleasant expression on her face. "Response to the changes we've made has been overwhelmingly positive."

He grunted and tapped the printout in front of him. "It says here Mason Banking has stopped advertising with us. They were our customers for twenty years."

"We've picked up other advertisers. Ones that are interested in the new demographic we're reaching." She leaned forward to look at the sheet he was studying. "You'll also see there that Glory Clothing company has contracted for the back cover, full color, for the next three months. Their account for one quarter is worth more than Mason Banking spent in a year."

His frown deepened. "I suppose they'll be ads featuring attractive, half-dressed young people who look as if they just fell out of bed."

She suppressed a smile. Maybe Gordon's problem was that he wasn't getting any. A girlfriend might do his disposition a world of good. "About the feature story for the next issue. I'm thinking of launching a series on different neighborhoods, starting with Montrose."

"Fine. I told you I don't object. Although I do think it's good to get back to an editorial subject matter. Artsy things like the photo-essay in this issue are fine for an occasional piece, but we don't want to get too weird."

She nodded, somehow managing to keep a straight face. Jake's photo-essay on public sculpture was already being talked about as award-worthy. And chief rival *Upscale Houston* was said to have their own photo piece in the works.

"Is that all you wanted to talk to me about?" he asked. "I'm very busy this morning."

"I won't keep you much longer." She crossed her legs, then uncrossed them, trying to appear calmer than she felt. She looked him in the eye, her gaze steady. "I need Glynna to write the Montrose piece."

Gordon was really scowling now. "Absolutely not."

Well, she hadn't expected him to give in easily, had

she? She'd come prepared to be as stubborn as he was. "She's the best writer we have on staff," she said. "In fact, the piece she wrote on the tunnel system was brilliant. It deserves to be printed."

Gordon pushed the printouts aside. "I believe I made myself clear on that issue. I have nothing more to say."

"It's obvious how you feel, but not why." She stood. "Look, Gordon, I realize Glynna is your daughter. But she's also a grown woman, and a very talented writer. Just because she happens to mention sex in a piece doesn't mean she's writing porn."

He shook his head. "It does her reputation no good to be seen as a writer of sexually oriented pieces."

She did smile now. It was so comical. "This is the twenty-first century. Not Victorian England. Glynna is an adult and she doesn't need you to protect her image."

"I am well aware of Glynna's age, and I don't delude myself into thinking she lives as a nun. But a young woman's reputation is still important and I won't see Glynna's sullied by questionable or sensational work." His eyes narrowed. "And I don't want her paired with that photographer again."

"Missy Thorpe?" Stacy pretended innocence. "Don't worry. Glynna didn't like working with her."

"Not her! That blond motorcycle fellow. Jack."

Stacy had no doubt Gordon knew "that blond motorcycle fellow's" name very well. He probably knew everything about Jake, including his shoe size. "You mean Jake Dawson. Unfortunately, he won't be with us much longer. He's leaving for New York soon."

"And good riddance. He's exactly the sort of man to turn a young woman's head."

"I don't think you give Glynna enough credit. She's always struck me as very sensible." She was walking close to the line right now, but she couldn't stop herself. Glynna was her friend and she deserved better than this sort of treatment. And the magazine deserved to have its best writer work on the cover story.

"Of course she's sensible. She's my daughter and I taught her well." He looked away. "But I've also sheltered her—perhaps too much."

"I know you're concerned," Stacy's voice was softer. "But you don't have to worry about Glynna."

He glanced at her. Did she imagine the regret she saw in his eyes? "You may think me overprotective, but I've always taken the responsibilities of raising a daughter very seriously."

"Then why do you treat her like a talentless child?" She stood, truly agitated now. "You criticize her work more than you do anyone else's. You give her *more* work than the other staff and you expect her to be at your beck and call."

He stared at her. "Under my tutelage, Glynna has learned every aspect of the operation of this magazine. She's well equipped to take over if something happens to me. As for criticizing her work, I've always urged her to do her best. Because of me, she's excelled in a very competitive field."

"But have you ever told her that?"

He stiffened. "It wouldn't do for her to become vain."

Stacy clenched her hands at her sides to keep from

reaching out and shaking him. "I know you didn't ask for my advice, and I'm probably out of line to give it. But you need to take a good look at your daughter and realize how wonderful she really is. She needs you to recognize that—and to tell her. Because if you don't, someone else is going to notice and appreciate her talent—and what a good person she is—and she's going to be gone. You won't have your best writer and your personal secretary anymore. And you may not even have a daughter."

"I think you've said enough, Ms. Southern."

"Yes, I think I have."

She turned and was at the door when his voice stopped her. "Ms. Southern—Stacy—even though I don't agree with what you have to say, I'm impressed that you have the strength of conviction to say it. Too few people stand up for their beliefs these days."

She bowed her head and took a deep breath. "Thank you, Gordon, but save your praise for Glynna. She needs to hear it."

She hurried away, before anger, or, heaven help her, tears, got the better of her. She needed to find Nick. He was the one person she could truly relax with. Nick allowed her to be vulnerable without making her feel weak. Nick would understand. Of all the things she'd gained from working at *Texas Style,* finding him had to be the best.

GLYNNA SLUMPED behind her desk and stared at the flower arrangement that had been waiting for her when she arrived this morning. Dahlias. Two dozen of them, in vivid pinks, purples and oranges. The wild, exotic blossoms she'd professed to liking that morning on the boat. The morning that had started it all.

There wasn't a card, but then, she didn't need one to know who had sent these. The question was, why? Why was Jake sending her flowers when things were over between them? Was he saying he was sorry? She hadn't seen him at all since that afternoon over a week ago when he'd found her in the parking garage. The next morning, she'd done as he'd suggested and sent the story about the tunnel system to *Upscale Houston.* That small act of rebellion had felt as exhilarating and terrifying as if she'd suddenly decided to change her name or move to another city. She should call him now and thank him for the flowers, and his encouragement. If nothing else, it would give her an excuse to talk to him again before he left town.

She reached up and felt the feathery-soft petals of an orange pom-pom blossom. The knowledge that he was leaving soon, if he hadn't already, had been a dull ache in her chest for days now. How much worse would she feel when he was really gone?

Unable to concentrate on work any longer, she went for lunch. She chose her favorite delicatessen and ate at a table by the window, forcing herself to focus on the passing scene, making up stories in her head about the people who strolled by. The exercise improved her mood somewhat, but Gordon's voice mail message that awaited her return sent her spirits plummeting once more. "Meet me in my office at 1:30," he ordered.

She frowned. Confrontations like this invariably consisted of him supplying long laundry lists of work for her to do, and/or lengthy critiques of some task she had not completed to his satisfaction. Rare praise was delivered in a brisk, dismissive tone that robbed her of any pleasure in the words.

Maybe I should look for another job, she thought as she stashed her purse in her desk. *At another magazine. Or in a different field altogether.*

She shook her head. She'd been raised from the cradle to work for *Texas Style.* She might as well try to change the color of her eyes.

She gathered up a notepad and pen and reported to her father's office. But this time, she promised herself if he asked her to do anything she didn't want to do, she'd stand up to him and refuse. And she'd tell him she wanted to write features again, too, along with some of the investigative pieces she had in mind.

He looked up when she entered and motioned to the chair across from him. "Close the door, Glynna, and sit down."

She did so, settling the notepad on her knees, her hands folded atop it. She kept her gaze focused on him. That had changed at least. A few months ago, she'd have sat with her head bowed, waiting for a verbal blow.

Gordon set aside the folder he'd been examining, then rearranged the pen lying alongside his blotter. He picked up his coffee cup, then set it aside again, avoiding looking at her.

Surprise bloomed in Glynna's chest. Her father was *fidgeting.* As if he was nervous about something. Gordon was never nervous. "Is something wrong?" she asked.

At last, he looked up at her. "Do you feel my treatment of you here at the office has been unduly harsh?"

The question startled her. What had brought this on? She shifted in her chair. "You expect a lot from everyone," she said.

"But I've always expected more from you. I won't deny that. I saw your talent early on and knew you had more to give."

Her mouth dropped open. She couldn't keep from staring at him. "You think I have talent?"

He sat up straighter. "You have tremendous talent. I never told you because I didn't want you to think too much of yourself. Even a gifted person must work hard to get ahead.".

"I've never minded hard work." She hesitated, then added. "But it would have meant a lot for me to hear that you thought I could write."

He suddenly looked older, his eyes sad. "I see now I was wrong to withhold my praise." He shook his head. "My only excuse is that in my experience, the business world is a place where slaps on the back are seldom given. I thought I was preparing you to succeed in that kind of environment."

A knot of tears choked her. The man before her now was the father she'd had when she was a little girl. Before her mother died and he closed himself off. She leaned toward him, her voice scarcely above a whisper. "What else haven't you told me?"

He looked down and ran his thumb along the edge of the blotter. "Do you...?" He cleared his throat and tried again. "Do you understand the reason I refused to run the feature you wrote on the tunnels?"

"I thought it was because you didn't like the way it was written. You said it sounded like a romance novel."

He frowned. "I was concerned what it would do for your reputation."

"I…I don't understand."

He cleared his throat again. "That piece, with its overtly sexual tone, following so closely on the two features on Paloma Island and the ship channel, would label you as a writer whose chief focus was sex."

She bit back a smile. It was touching really. And quite ridiculous. "Do you think there's something wrong with sex?"

He flushed. "No. There's a time and place for it, certainly. But I don't think a young woman—"

"I'm twenty-six years old." She smiled, unable to resist teasing him. "And I have had sex. I quite enjoyed it." Would she ever enjoy it as much again as she had with Jake? The thought was like a pinprick to the bubble of happiness that had swelled within her.

Gordon's face was crimson now. He took a long drink from his coffee cup. "I know you're saying these things to shock me. Perhaps because you think I need shocking. Perhaps I do." He looked at her again, his gaze softer. "It isn't an easy thing for a father to admit that his little girl is all grown-up. Especially when I've raised you by myself." He knotted his fingers together. "I'm reluctant to see you mature and change."

She reached out and put her hand on his. How much had it taken him to make such an admission? "Growing up doesn't have to mean growing apart," she said. "And change isn't always for the worse."

He nodded. "I've done a lot of thinking recently. And I can see some of my ideas may have been wrong. While my intentions were honorable, you bore the brunt of my mistakes."

Noble-sounding words. But what did they mean? She waited.

He cleared his throat. "I've decided to hire a personal secretary. There's no need for you to fill that position. Frankly, it's a waste of your talent."

She stared at him. Was this a good thing, or bad? She'd never liked being his flunky, but did this mean he didn't want her around anymore? "I don't know what to say."

"I've also decided to ask for your appointment to our board of directors. That way you'll have a more direct say in the company's affairs."

All the breath rushed out of her. She collapsed against the back of the chair. Long ago she'd assumed she wouldn't have a role in running the magazine until Gordon was gone. "I…I'm honored."

He nodded, some of the strain around his eyes and mouth easing. "Finally, I've decided—and in fact, Stacy has demanded—that you return to your position as chief feature writer. And I want to run your piece on the tunnels as the cover story for the next issue."

She felt truly faint now, afraid she might slide to the floor.

"What is it?" He leaned toward her. "Are you ill?"

She couldn't look at him. She clenched her fists,

steeling herself for his rage. "When you refused to run the story, I...I thought it was too good to stick in a drawer, so I sent it to another magazine."

She could feel him glaring at her. "What magazine?"

"U-Upscale Houston."

In the silence that followed, she could hear the mechanical ticking of his desk clock, and the rush of wind as the air-conditioning kicked on. She gripped the arms of the chair until her knuckles ached, and forced herself to raise her head and look at him.

"What did they think of it?" he asked, his voice devoid of emotion.

She took a deep breath. "They're going to publish it in their next issue."

He rose, looming over her. "So as soon as I refused to run the story, you decided to get back at me by sending it to our chief competitor?" All tenderness vanished as his all-too-familiar temper took its place. "Never mind that I was trying to keep you from making a mistake. How could you betray everything I've worked for this way? I thought I could depend on you to be more loyal than that."

At one time, such criticism would have crippled her, but all the risks she'd taken in her personal life these past months had made her more confident, more sure of her own worth. Long-dormant anger swelled at Gordon's harsh words. She stood and looked him in the eye. "You told me you didn't want the piece. You didn't want *me*."

He drew back, and she allowed herself a flicker of triumph.

"I was trying to protect you," he said.

"I don't need protecting. I'm not a helpless little girl anymore."

"You're obviously not the daughter I raised, either."

He turned away. She stared at his back, wanting to scream at him, to make him turn around. But what good would it do? She'd tried for too many years to be the daughter he wanted—a woman who didn't exist. Now she knew the only way she'd ever be happy was to be herself—not a society lady or a ruthless businesswoman or slavishly devoted offspring. Just—Glynna. Flaws and faults and all.

She turned and ran from the office. In the hallway, she collided with someone. Strong arms encircled her. "Glynna, what is it? What's wrong?" Jake asked.

She couldn't talk to him right now. Not when she hurt so much. Being with him would remind her all over again that he was leaving and that would be too much to bear.

She pushed him away. "I'll be fine." Then she ran, into her office, where she locked the door and gave herself up to grieving for all the things that might have been. With her father, and with Jake.

JAKE DEBATED whether to go after Glynna. She'd literally been trembling, she'd been so upset. What had happened to her? He looked down the hallway, in the direction from which she'd come. The only thing down that way was the publisher's office. Of course. He clenched his jaw. Only her father could have upset Glynna so much.

He pushed into Gordon's office without knocking. The publisher was slumped behind his desk, head in his hands. At Jake's approach, he straightened. "What do you want?" he demanded.

"What's wrong with Glynna? Why did she run out of here looking so upset?"

Gordon's glare would have withered a lesser man. "That is none of your concern."

Jake planted his hands on the desk and leaned over the older man. Only Gordon's age saved him from being jerked out of the chair and shaken. "Somebody needs to be concerned about her since you obviously aren't."

"You know nothing about my daughter and me. Leave my office at once." Gordon pointed toward the door.

Jake shook his head. "No. Not until you tell me why she was upset. What did you say or do to her?"

"*I* didn't do anything. She's the one who sold a feature story to *Upscale Houston.* Our chief competitor."

So they'd bought the story. Disappointment pinched at him when he realized she hadn't shared the news with him. "The tunnel story?"

Gordon's eyes narrowed. "How did you know?"

Jake stood up. "Good for her. It's a great piece."

"How did you know she submitted it to them?"

"I suggested she send it."

"You did what?" Gordon half rose from his chair.

"You rejected it. She was going to stick it in a drawer until I pointed out you don't run all the magazines in the city. It was a good story. It deserved to be printed and she deserved recognition for writing it."

Gordon collapsed into the chair again, though he continued to glower at Jake. "What is your relationship with my daughter?"

Lover wasn't the right word anymore. *Friend?* They were more than that, weren't they? "I care about her," he said at last. "I don't like to see her hurt."

"You have no business caring about her."

Fresh anger lanced through him. "Somebody has to."

Gordon launched himself out of the chair and leaned over the desk, his face mottled with rage. "You're fired! Get out of here."

"You can't fire me. I already quit." He turned and left, afraid of what he might do if he stayed any longer. His pulse pounded at his temples and his heart raced. To think Glynna had to put up with a man like that for a father.

To think Jake was leaving her to face Gordon alone.

The thought made him sick to his stomach. He hurried to his office and began emptying the drawers into an empty copy paper box. He had to get out of here before he made things worse.

A noise in the doorway stopped him. He turned and was surprised to see Glynna. She'd stopped crying, though her eyes were red. "What are you doing?" she asked, looking at the box.

"I'm leaving."

"Right now?"

He looked around the mostly empty office. "No time like the present." Gordon had made it clear he didn't want him around.

"So you're going?"

He tossed a desk clock into the box. "Yep. The sooner I'm out of here, the better." If he ran into Gordon again, he was liable to punch him in the jaw.

She stared at him a moment, then turned and left. He

looked after her, debating going to comfort her, then shook his head. She was still upset about her father. Maybe the best thing was to give her time to get it together on her own.

As he emptied the last of the desk drawers, he told himself it was time he cleared out this office anyway. He'd already put off leaving for New York for two weeks, telling himself he needed to finish assignments and make all the arrangements here. But the truth was, he was having second thoughts about leaving. New York had been his goal for so long, but up close, it didn't look so attractive. He had it good here—regular clients, a gallery that carried his work, friends.

New York had a lot of things, but it didn't have Glynna. That was the real problem; it hurt to admit it. He'd always prided himself on never letting a woman get in the way of what he wanted. Now the least likely woman had taken hold of his heart. Could it be that love-'em-and-leave-'em Jake Dawson had finally found a woman he couldn't walk away from?

17

STACY STAYED at her desk until six, but headed straight to Nick's apartment after work. The art director always left the office promptly at five, but his department ran as smoothly as any at the magazine. How did he manage that? She'd have to ask him some time, but right now, she had more important things on her mind.

His car was in the parking lot, so she knew he was home, but when he hadn't answered by the third ring, she was debating getting the manager to let her in. They didn't have any time to waste.

Then the door opened and there he was, his chest bare, tight jeans hugging his hips and thighs. Her breath caught, and every word she'd been prepared to say vanished from her thoughts. She could only stare, melting from the inside out.

He smiled, a roguish grin that kicked her temperature up another notch. "This is a nice surprise." He pulled her into the apartment, up against his chest, and kissed her with slow intensity. It was the kiss of a man who is thoroughly at ease with the territory he's exploring, a kiss meant to derive every enjoyment from that familiarity.

lung to him, her knees on the verge of buckling, er senses foggy. She could forget everything when she was with Nick. The knowledge was both dangerous and appealing.

Reluctantly, she broke away, grabbing hold of the back of a chair to keep from falling. "We don't have time for that now, Nick."

"Oh?" He arched one eyebrow, a devilish, teasing expression that was so appealing she had to look away. But she couldn't ignore his hands, which grasped her waist and dragged her close once more. "I always have time for you, baby."

What woman doesn't want to hear *those* words? Exactly why was she here? She grasped his arms, stilling his roving fingers. "Don't think I'm not tempted, but right now we have something more important to do."

"What could be more important?" He leaned over and nibbled her neck.

She stifled a groan. "Some things take precedence over sex."

"It's more than just sex when I'm with you, and you know it."

The words raised a lump of emotion in her throat. She leaned in to him, surrendering for a second to the exquisite feel of his mouth on her. It *was* more than mere physical gratification when she was with Nick. He understood her.

"We have to help Glynna and Jake," she managed to gasp, as his hand moved to cup her breast.

He grew still and raised his head, frowning. "What's wrong with Glynna and Jake?"

"I'm not sure." She took advantage of his distraction to move away from him, to the other side of the chair. "You know my office is near Gordon's. I heard Glynna arguing with him this afternoon. She left his office, very upset, and the next think I know, *Jake's* in Gordon's office, and *they're* shouting at each other."

"What about?"

"When Gordon vetoed Glynna's tunnel story, she turned around and sold it to *Upscale Houston.*"

Nick whistled. "That took some balls."

She smoothed her hand along the back of the chair. "I'm not happy about losing the piece, but I don't blame Glynna. It deserved to be published. And she needs to get recognition from someone who appreciates her. Which is basically what Jake told Gordon."

"No wonder Gordon was pissed."

"He fired Jake."

Nick shook his head. "It doesn't matter, since he was leaving anyway."

"And he's a fool if he does."

Nick stepped back, his surprise at her vehemence evident. "What do you mean? Jake's got a great chance in New York. He'd be an idiot not to take it."

She shook her head and knotted her hands together. "He wouldn't have come to Glynna's defense if he didn't care about her. And I know she cares for him."

Nick put his hands on her shoulders. "How do you know that? Jake admitted to me they'd been involved, but he was clear on the past tense. Whatever they had, it's over."

"No, it's not." She looked into his eyes. "I've seen

them together. The way they look at each other. They *do* still care. They're just too scared to admit it."

His smile was tender. "Did anyone ever tell you for such a tough broad, you have a soft heart?"

"We'll keep it our secret." She spread her hands flat on his chest, savoring the warmth of his skin. "Will you help me?"

"What are we supposed to do? Kidnap the two of them and lock them in a room together?"

"Not a bad idea, but I had something less drastic in mind first."

"What's that?"

She pressed one finger to his mouth. "Let's try talking to them. You know, old-fashioned communication."

"I've always been a fan of communication without words." He kissed her neck, the heat of his lips rolling through her like a wave.

"I know you artists and your disdain for words." She forced herself to push him away.

He laughed. "All right. We'll try it your way first. Let me get dressed."

"Hurry."

He paused on his way to the bedroom and turned to her again. "There's just one thing I want to know."

"What's that?"

"I know Glynna's your friend, but—why are you so set on getting her back together with Jake?"

A blush crept over her cheeks, but she kept her gaze focused on him. "Because I want Glynna to have what I have with you."

Another man might have panicked at the words, or

laughed them off, but Nick did neither. He gave her a long, considering look, and happiness leapt in her like a flame. "Yeah," he said, his voice rough. "I see what you mean."

GLYNNA FROZE when she heard the doorbell. She did *not* want to see anyone today. Not when she looked like a hag from crying and she had chocolate smeared down the front of her blouse from her futile attempt to drown her sorrows in a pint of rocky road.

The bell sounded again, long and insistent. She sniffed and scrubbed at her eyes with a wadded tissue. If she ignored whoever it was, maybe they'd go away. She was in no mood to smile and pretend interest in some Girl Scout's sales pitch or evangelist's attempt to save her soul.

Whoever was on the other side of the door gave up ringing the bell and began knocking. Hard. It definitely sounded like a man. Her heart climbed into her throat. Had Jake come to see her? To say goodbye?

The thought made her want to dive headfirst into a whole *vat* of rocky road.

"Glynna, open up. We know you're in there."

A woman's voice—Stacy?—startled Glynna. She went to the door and peered out the peephole. Nick stared back at her, the fish-eye lens distorting his face into a fun-house vision. Stacy stood behind him, arms folded across her chest, one toe rapidly tapping the floor.

With a sigh, Glynna unfastened the chain and locks and pulled open the door. "What are you two doing here?" She kept her head turned away, hoping they wouldn't see she'd been crying.

"We came to see if you were all right," Nick said.

"And to try to talk some sense into you." Stacy walked past them, into the kitchen of the condo. She frowned at the empty ice-cream carton in the sink and the half liter of Diet Coke open on the counter. "All this is going to get you is another inch on your thighs." She turned to face Glynna once more. "What happened to upset you so much? I overhead you arguing with your father."

"Now you know the truth, Stacy's an eavesdropper." Nick put his hand on Glynna's shoulder and steered her toward the couch.

Stacy followed them. "I couldn't help but hear the shouting."

Glynna nodded. "It's okay. Eavesdropping is an occupational hazard for writers." She glanced at Nick. "We can't help it. Nosiness is pretty much bred in us."

He nodded. "Just like artists are voyeurs."

A tremor danced down her spine at his words, and she heard, not Nick's voice, but Jake's. *Every photographer is a voyeur at heart.*

"I take it Gordon was upset about your selling the tunnel article to *Upscale Houston.*"

She sniffed. "I…I don't know if I really blame him. They're our biggest competitor. I guess I can see how he'd think I'd betrayed him."

"That's ridiculous. He'd already refused to run the article in *Texas Style.* The piece was too good not publish."

She nodded. "That's what Jake said, too." She swallowed fresh tears. "It hurts that my father always thinks the worst of me."

"It's not just you," Nick said. "Gordon's a pessimist at heart."

Stacy sat beside Glynna on the sofa and took her hand. "I know you've pretty much grown up at the magazine, and it's been in your family for years and everything, but have you ever thought of working somewhere else?"

She bit her lip, counting on the pain to clear her head and drive away tears. "I guess I'll have to now," she said. "My father fired me."

"You're talented enough to work anywhere." Nick leaned back against the bar and crossed his arms over his chest. "I know people at other mags around the state. I'd be happy to make some calls."

"I'd be willing to call people, too," Stacy hurried to add. She squeezed Glynna's hand. "It might be a good thing for you, to get out from under your father's thumb and find out what you can really do."

Was the fluttering in her stomach nerves, or excitement? Could she really find a job somewhere else, some place where her work counted more than her name? The thought was terrifying—and exhilarating. She looked from Nick to Stacy and back. "I've never thought much before about what I wanted to do. From the time I could read, I just assumed I'd work at *Texas Style.*"

"And you may come back yet," Stacy said.

"Might be good to see how things are done at other places, then bring that experience back to the family business, so to speak," Nick said.

Glynna nodded. What they said made sense, if only she had the courage to do so. That was one quality she seemed to have in short supply these days. Maybe she'd used it all up seducing Jake.

Thinking of him, she had to duck her head to hide threatening tears. Stacy's arm slipped around her shoulders. "What is it? What's really bugging you?"

She shook her head. Stacy was a sophisticated, experienced woman who probably never had trouble with men. If the looks he was sending her direction were any indication, Nick was certainly under her sway. She'd probably laugh at the idea of someone like Glynna going after a guy like Jake.

Stacy sat back and studied her. "It's Jake Dawson, isn't it?"

Glynna gasped and looked up. "Wh—why do you say that?"

"Apparently, Jake and your old man had a few words this afternoon, too." Nick crossed to the sofa and sat on her other side. "About you."

"Jake and my father argued about me?" She looked at Stacy for confirmation of this.

The editor nodded. "Apparently, Jake overheard, or figured out, what happened between you and Gordon and he confronted him. He defended your decision to sell the article and really raked Gordon over the coals for not treating you better."

Her heart beat like an uncoordinated drummer. "He did that?"

Stacy smiled. "He told your father he cared about you and wouldn't stand for your being hurt."

"Oh, my." She looked at her clenched hands in her lap. "What did my father do?"

"He fired Jake."

She frowned. "But…if Jake's leaving anyway…"

"I know. It makes no sense," Nick said. "If I know Jake, he told your old man he quit."

"So when I saw him cleaning out his office…"

"What else could he do?" Stacy said. "Whether he quit or was fired, he had to clear out."

"I guess it doesn't matter." She swallowed hard. "I imagine he'll be leaving for New York in a few days anyway."

"I don't know about that." Nick shook his head.

She stared at him. "What do you mean?"

He shrugged. "Just that he's clearly stalling. From what I understand, his friend wanted him up there two weeks ago, but Jake keeps finding excuses to stay." His eyes met hers, one brow quirked questioningly.

She looked away. "I guess he had a lot to do. Assignments to finish…and things like that."

"I think a certain brunette is keeping him here," Stacy said.

If only that were the truth. Glynna shook her head. "Jake's always dreamed about going to New York. He won't let anything stop him."

Stacy blew out a breath in frustration. "Okay, this is none of my business, but I can't stand it anymore. What is going on between you two?"

"Nothing." At least not anymore. Their fling was officially over, though Glynna would live with the repercussions for a long time to come. She'd set out to explore her wild side and found her heart tamed by a man she couldn't have.

"Did anyone ever tell you you're a lousy liar?" Nick's smile softened the sting of his words.

"I've seen the way you and Jake look at each other," Stacy said. "As if you can't keep your hands off each other."

Glynna blushed. "Maybe once. But that's over now."

"Then why did Jake pull the photos he took of you from his show?"

She whirled to face Nick. "What? How did you know about those?"

"Relax." He leaned forward, hands on his knees. "Terrence, the guy who owns the gallery, is a friend of mine. He knew I know Jake, and he called me in a panic, saying Jake was pulling his best work from the show. It was bad enough he'd refused to sell any of the photos— Terrence couldn't stand that he was keeping his best work a secret. When he told me they were of a dark-haired woman, and that Jake said they were 'personal,' I put two and two together."

"He pulled the photos from the show?"

"He must have done it to avoid embarrassing you," Stacy said. "Or maybe because those images were too private for him to share."

"Oh, no." She buried her face in her hands, trying to force her muddled thoughts into coherence. She'd accused Jake of using her for his own gain, and instead, he'd put her wishes ahead of his own ambition. "Why would he have done such a thing?"

Stacy touched her arm. "Honey, I think Jake's in love with you."

She shook her head. "That can't be."

"Why is it so hard to believe?" Stacy slipped her arm around her once more and hugged her close. "I can't think of anyone better for him to love."

Hope made her giddy, as if she'd drunk too much champagne. Did Jake really love her? What would he say if she told him she loved him too? Would words really change anything? Her elation vanished, and the pain hit her hard all over again. "Even if it's true, it doesn't change things. Jake's going to New York. I'm staying here. End of story."

"So write a new ending."

Both women stared at Nick. He grinned. "Don't look so surprised. Just because I'm an art director doesn't mean I can't occasionally think like a journalist. Haven't you ever rewritten a story before?"

"But…how could I do that?" Glynna asked.

"Go to him," Stacy urged. "Tell him how you feel. How you *really* feel."

Did she have the courage to do that? Could she lay her heart bare for Jake, knowing that he might very well reject her? Could she stand having the two most important men in her life both turn her away? "I'll have to think about it," she said after a moment.

"What's to think about? I say—"

Nick pulled Stacy up off the couch, silencing her in midsentence. "We have to go now."

"But I'm not—"

Still smiling, he tugged her toward the door. "I think we've done enough. The rest is up to Glynna."

Stacy looked back at Glynna, who stood and managed a small smile. "Thank you both for stopping by," she said. "I really appreciate it." She sighed. "You've given me a lot to think about."

"Call if you need anything." Stacy leaned into Nick and he hugged her close. "Anything."

"I will. I promise." She walked them out, marveling at how different Stacy was with Nick. Softer. As if she wasn't afraid to let her guard down.

Could Glynna be that vulnerable with Jake?

She sniffed, then gave up and blew her nose. She had to try. If she didn't, she might as well crawl back to her father, beg forgiveness and return to being the dutiful daughter and resident doormat. Jake had helped her climb out of that role. If nothing else, she owed it to him—and to herself—not to go back there.

Clinging to this sliver of determination, she headed for the shower. She had a couple of calls to make and she wasn't about to show up looking this bad. She was going to look like a confident, successful woman no matter what doubts still lingered in her head.

18

As GLYNNA STOOD in the doorway of her father's office, she realized how long it had been since she'd really looked at him. It shocked her now, to see how old he was, the pink scalp showing through his thinning hair, his fingers like claws as he buried his face in his hands. Her heart twisted, and she thought of all the time they'd both wasted, not really paying attention to one another.

She cleared her throat, and he looked up, startled. At the sight of her, he sat up, and smoothed his hands across the book open in front of him. "Come in, Glynna," he said.

"I stopped by the house first, but when I didn't find you there I came here." She stopped in front of the desk and nodded to the volumes stacked at his elbow. "What are you looking at?"

"Old issues of *Texas Style*. From when your grandfather ran the publication." He turned the volume in front of him to face her, and pointed to a photo of a stunning woman in a smart suit. "This is your mother when she was about your age."

Glynna hadn't seen this picture before, though she'd seen others from that era. Her mother had also written for the magazine. Here she was accepting an award, smiling for the camera, twin dimples at the corners of her mouth, like her daughter, brown eyes shining. Glynna's eyes burned and she thought again how unfair it was that she had never gotten to know her mother. What advice would she have given Glynna today, about Gordon, and about Jake?

Gordon turned the book back. "Why were you looking for me?"

She sat, pulling the leather side chair close to the desk. "We need to talk."

The lines around his eyes and mouth deepened. He clenched his hands together atop the book. "Some things were said this afternoon that shouldn't have been."

She tentatively put her hand on his, wanting to make that connection. "I can see how you would think my selling to *Upscale Houston* was a betrayal, but it wasn't meant that way."

He nodded. "I know that. It's hard for an old man to admit he's wrong." He looked at her mother's picture again. "After she died, I promised myself I would raise you to be a woman she'd be proud of. When I saw how much you loved writing, I realized you could become the success your mother never had the chance to be."

She swallowed. "I've read some of her work. She was very talented."

He met her eyes at last, some of the weariness receded. "You have her gift. I thought making you work hard and teaching you to be tough would make you a competitor. Someone who would be recognized one day as the top in your field." He looked away again. "But when the time came that I knew you'd developed enough to make it on your own, I couldn't bear to let you go."

The top in your field. The thought made her weak. Did he really think she was that good? She tightened her hand on his. "What do you mean?"

He pulled away, and leaned back in his chair, studying her. "You've done everything you can here at the magazine. You need a bigger playing field now. More challenges. It's time I admitted that."

She nodded, trying to rein in the giddiness that threatened to run away with her. "I've been thinking it might be good for me to go away for a while. To work somewhere else. That doesn't mean I wouldn't come back here some time," she hastened to add.

He nodded. "I hope you would want to keep the business in the family." He glanced at her mother's picture again. "I think she would have wanted it."

"I agree. But seeing how other publications operate, learning new things and gleaning fresh ideas, will help me when it's my turn to take a larger hand in running things here. Which I hope won't happen for a long time."

"Sooner than you think, I'm afraid." He smiled. "It seems like only yesterday you were a little girl, playing on the floor here in this very office while I worked. I'd give you paper and a pen and you'd write stories. Even then, you told me you were going to be a reporter and work for me."

Memory flooded her, clogging her throat with tears. She hadn't thought of those days in years. She and her father had been really close then, almost inseparable.

She'd spent hours after school "working" with him, and every evening they'd sit on the sofa after supper and read or watch TV. What had happened to drive them so far apart?

"I meant what I said earlier, about putting you on the board. It's past time that was done."

She swallowed past the tightness she felt and nodded. "I'm honored."

"Where will you go?"

"I'm not sure." The thought of striking out on her own made her weak at the knees, but she was a braver woman now than she'd been even a few months ago. She could do it.

"If there's anything you need, you know you have my support." He rose, pushing up slowly from the desk. "I know I haven't offered it enough, but I'm man enough to admit when I'm wrong and try to mend my ways."

She stood also, and came around the desk to slip her arm in his. "Not many men would have had the courage to turn the magazine around the way you have. I admired the way you let Stacy make some pretty radical changes, even if they went against your own thinking."

"She called me a hide-bound dinosaur."

Glynna choked back a laugh and squeezed his arm. "And you let her."

He coughed. "No woman has stood up to me that way since your mother. And she had a point." He glanced at her. "You've got your mother's spirit, too, you know. I haven't given you much chance to show it off, but it's managed to come out on its own these past few weeks."

She smiled. "Yes, it has." She hugged him close. "I

love you, Dad," she whispered. It felt good to say those words. They'd been trapped inside her too long.

"I love you too, Pumpkin."

At the sound of this pet name, not heard since childhood, tears trickled down her cheeks. She struggled not to lose it altogether. Somehow, collapsing in sobs would spoil the moment.

Silently, he handed her a handkerchief and patted her shoulder while she dabbed at her eyes. "Everything will be all right," he said. "You'll see. We'll make it right."

She nodded. Despite everything, she believed his words were true. She'd stepped over a threshold today. She wasn't sure what lay ahead of her, but she knew now she had it in her to come out on top. She had her mother's talent, and her father's strength, to see her through.

JAKE STRETCHED a band of tape across the top of the last carton of books and shoved it aside. With everything relegated to boxes, the apartment had a forlorn look about it. His steps echoed as he moved through the rooms. In the morning he'd ship the last of the things he couldn't live without to his temporary address in New York. This afternoon, the movers were coming to cart everything else to storage.

He should have been full of energy, excited about this move he'd waited for so long. Instead, fatigue dragged at him. He felt drained. And dreaded the prospect of starting over in a new place.

He picked up his cell phone from the kitchen counter, then laid it back down. He needed to call

Glynna, but what would he say? Goodbye was too final, and it didn't tell her anything about how he really felt. Could he say what was in his heart without breaking down? And would it make any difference in the end?

The doorbell rang and frowning, he went to answer it. If that was the movers, they were early. They'd just have to wait until...

He stared at Glynna for a long moment. Even distorted by the fish-eye lens of the peephole, the sight of her made his heart race. He rushed the turn the locks and jerk open the door. "I didn't expect to see you here," he said.

"You didn't?" She smiled and walked past him into the apartment, carrying two suitcases. "I thought I'd surprise you."

He followed, half-sick to his stomach. "Are you taking a trip?" he asked.

She set the luggage down and turned to face him. "I've quit my job at the magazine."

He nodded. "I take it Gordon was pretty upset over the tunnel piece."

She waved the words away. "Oh, we've straightened that all out. He apologized and everything."

He stared at her. "Gordon apologized?"

She laughed. "I know he comes off as a fire-breathing dragon, but underneath, he's not so bad. He and I had a long talk and cleared up a lot of misunderstandings. We both agreed it will do me good to get some experience elsewhere, at least for a while."

"What are you going to do now?" He glanced again at the suitcases.

"I have some money saved and a folder full of half-written stories, so I thought I'd try freelancing for a while. See where that takes me."

"So…where are you going?"

Her dimples deepened as she beamed at him. "I was thinking New York. Do you want to share a cab to the airport?"

He didn't let himself stop to think this time. For once he pushed reason and planning aside and acted on pure emotion. He reached her in two strides, and drew her close. "What would you say to sharing more than a cab?" He cradled her cheek, his hand trembling.

She leaned into his palm, rubbing her face against his calloused skin. "What are you suggesting?"

"I already have an apartment rented. We could share."

She straightened and looked him in the eye. "You're asking me to be your roommate?"

He winced. He was making a mess of this. "More than a roommate," he said. "If you'll have me."

She frowned and pushed away from him. "I need words, Jake. The right ones."

He ducked his head, and took a deep breath. She was right. She deserved words. And pictures and gestures and dammit, he'd break into song if he had to. Instead, he took both her hands in his, holding on for strength as much as anything else. "Glynna, I love you," he said. "And all the success in the world won't mean anything if you're not there to share it with me."

She nodded. "I like what I hear so far. Go on."

He swallowed hard. All he wanted was to pull her close and kiss her until they were both breathless, to *show* her how much he loved her, in a way mere words could never convey.

But she wanted words. Fine. He'd give them to her. Every corny, clichéd one, if that's what it took. Still holding her hands, he sank to his knees amid the boxes and gazed up at her, encouraged by the sudden softness in her eyes. "Glynna McCormick, will you marry me?" he asked. "I want to spend the rest of my life photographing you."

"Oh, Jake!" She fell to her knees, and into his arms. "Yes," she whispered, kissing his forehead, his eyes, his cheeks. "Yes. Yes." Their lips met, warm and tender, and then more urgent, love words interspersed with kisses, their hands squeezing, touching, as if discovering each other all over again. They stretched out on the carpet and Jake rolled over onto his back, pulling her on top of him. He smiled up at her. "I'll never get tired of looking at you," he said. "Of touching you." He smoothed his hand down her back.

"I'll never get tired of loving you," she said. "I think I knew it that first night we were together." She rested her head on his chest.

"You mean the night you seduced me?"

"I didn't seduce you."

"Yes, you did. Shy little Glynna McCormick came on to me on the beach."

She giggled, the sound vibrating through him. "And what did you think?"

"That there was a lot more to you than I expected." He moved his hand down to cup her bottom. "Things I want to spend a lifetime discovering."

She wiggled closer, every movement sharpening his desire. She nipped at his neck, her tongue hot against his flesh. "Jake?"

"Uh-huh?" He slid his hand up her skirt, enjoying the feel of her silk-covered bottom.

"What would you say if I said I wanted to seduce you again?" She unfastened the top button of his shirt.

"Mmm. I'd say I'll give you, oh, fifty years or so to stop."

Her fingers rapidly worked the buttons, and spread the shirt apart to bare his chest. "What time does your plane leave?"

"Not until tomorrow."

"Then we've got lots of time."

He started to tell her about the movers, but then she drew his nipple into her mouth and his mind fogged. There'll be time for talk later. And if the movers arrived in the meantime... Well, they'd just have to wait.

If you enjoyed what you just read,
then we've got an offer you can't resist!

Take 2 bestselling love stories FREE!

Plus get a FREE surprise gift!

Clip this page and mail it to **Harlequin Reader Service**®

IN U.S.A.	IN CANADA
3010 Walden Ave.	P.O. Box 609
P.O. Box 1867	Fort Erie, Ontario
Buffalo, N.Y. 14240-1867	L2A 5X3

YES! Please send me 2 free Blaze™ novels and my free surprise gift. After receiving them, if I don't wish to receive anymore, I can return the shipping statement marked cancel. If I don't cancel, I will receive 4 brand-new novels each month, before they're available in stores! In the U.S.A., bill me at the bargain price of $3.99 plus 25¢ shipping and handling per book and applicable sales tax, if any*. In Canada, bill me at the bargain price of $4.47 plus 25¢ shipping and handling per book and applicable taxes**. That's the complete price and a savings of at least 10% off the cover prices—what a great deal! I understand that accepting the 2 free books and gift places me under no obligation ever to buy any books. I can always return a shipment and cancel at any time. Even if I never buy another book from Harlequin, the 2 free books and gift are mine to keep forever.

150 HDN DZ9K
350 HDN DZ9L

Name	(PLEASE PRINT)	
Address	Apt.#	
City	State/Prov.	Zip/Postal Code

Not valid to current Harlequin Blaze™ subscribers.

Want to try two free books from another series?
Call 1-800-873-8635 or visit www.morefreebooks.com.

 * Terms and prices subject to change without notice. Sales tax applicable in N.Y.
** Canadian residents will be charged applicable provincial taxes and GST.
   All orders subject to approval. Offer limited to one per household.
 ® and ™ are registered trademarks owned and used by the trademark owner and or its licensee.

BLZ04R   ©2004 Harlequin Enterprises Limited.

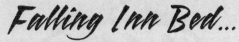